**WHAT BOOKS PRESS**

AN IMPRINT OF

THE GLASS TABLE

COLLECTIVE

LOS ANGELES

# THE
# PERSISTENCE

# THE
# PERSISTENCE

STORIES

JOHN COLBURN

WHAT
BOOKS
PRESS

LOS ANGELES

Library of Congress Cataloging-in-Publication Data
Names: Colburn, John (John Allen), 1967- author
Title: The persistence : stories / John Colburn.
Description: Los Angeles : What Books Press, 2025. | Summary: "The force
    beneath creation surfaces in ten linked stories that twist through
    numerous realities. Characters return or depart across a boundary that
    barely holds back possibilities for the monstrous. In the patch of feral
    woods in which these stories are set, the covering over the generative
    void is exceptionally thin, allowing the poetry of being to appear in
    bizarre ways."-- Provided by publisher.
Identifiers: LCCN 2025030371 | ISBN 9798998905506 paperback
Subjects: LCGFT: Short stories
Classification: LCC PS3603.O417 P47 2025 | DDC 813/.6--dc23/eng/20250902
LC record available at https://lccn.loc.gov/2025030371

Cover art: Gronk, *Untitled*, mixed media on paper, 2024
Book design by ash good, www.ashgood.com

What Books Press
363 South Topanga Canyon Boulevard
Topanga, CA 90290

WHATBOOKSPRESS.COM

*this book is for Lois Kittleson*
(1916–1990)

# CONTENTS

summer story                                    5

the two daughters                               16

how I became a mother                           24

the story of the box                            31

the weeper                                      43

the story of henry ford                         71

brother and sister                              82

the story of eating the king                   112

the story of the miracles                      121

the western story                              135


acknowledgments                                154

*once more I'm the nothing that imagines you*

—Victor Rodriguez Nunez


*"The Nothing is our main care," said Reb Idar.*
*"We often sacrifice to it the finest hours*
*we hoped for."*

—Edmond Jabés

# SUMMER STORY

I WANT TO tell you about the boredom of reading comic books in the hot summer house and the smell of the yellowed pages and baking maple floorboards and the wind in the oak trees and the town itself an island of empty porches and rusted flat-tire cars and metallic clanging from the gas station up the block and the palpable nothing at all floating across playgrounds shimmering with heat and no people, just the emptiness of hot summer drifting inside a pressure planet, a nowhere, and the comic book filled with busty women and bright colors is not even a thing, is just a piece of time that smells hot. It's too hot to play a record. It's too hot to shoot baskets. Glass of lemonade sweating a ring onto the nightstand and there's nothing to do. There's nothing. The unbearable creak of the bed as you kick your legs. The radio voice in the passing car and how it fades up the street, how it irritates. You waited all school year for this and now time has stopped. Your parents don't believe in air conditioning for just two weeks of heat in the goddamn summer.

You want to have sex but you don't want to have sex, you want to fantasize about having sex and you know you're not ready but maybe you are or can imagine how it will be when you are ready or to hell with ready what does that even mean, what if you did it anyway, are you afraid or not, that thrill of touching a girl in the swimming pool, of feeling each other up, paused near the ladder, how strange it felt when she put her hand between your legs and you laughed and touched her too, but today there's nothing. A comic book and a glass of lemonade and the sound of a lawnmower. There's really nothing to do in the universe, the all-around emptiness. There is only fantasy. Why grow up and just do nothing and work and be like your parents.

You go downstairs. It's just too hot. You go out the back door and across what feels like the burning surface of the sun, the impossible bright yard, squinting, this planet not suitable for human habitation, you are halfway toward an erection, the bicycle leaning against the garage with its metallic gold banana seat and the grass half brown now at the start of August. There's nothing to do but get on the bicycle and ride the streets looking for jumps, a mindless boy in the middle of a mindless stretch of prairie where no people should make permanent dwellings.

Empty side streets, some cars parked in driveways and patches of street tar soft to the touch, who cares about love, you might explode, you jump the bike into the air just to disconnect for a free moment, a little animal whirling through the heat to land in the brittle grass and there's gravity dragging you along and there's sweat and there's time squeezing in. You bike right into the gas station with fifty cents for the coke machine and how those men can make you feel weak when they're changing tires and moving slowly beneath the cars laughing and they don't look at you. Those fucking men.

Another boy, long hair and no shirt, bikes up to the coke machine. The handlebars on his bicycle are broken on one side. Chad. You don't like him, of course it would be Chad, he moved here from where, Ohio? And you think what's worse, nothing or this.

"Hey."
"What's up."

Shrug.

"Wanna ride to the park?"

"OK."

The park waves too in the heat and the monkey bars and the slow river monotonous and edged with slime. The erection and the comic book women and the feeling of future sex almost gone but also present, at the outline edge of every gesture. Those muscular women in skin-tight uniforms who can fly or shoot arrows or bolts of lightning or walk through walls.

Chad whips back his long hair. He rides down the ditch near the park and jumps up the other side, both wheels off the ground, vaulting over the sidewalk. You follow in a clumsy show of courage. Stoic. What do you want. What do you want.

The river at least cools your body and you find crayfish that will battle each other to death in the green slick stones. But the river is slow at the dry end of summer. Every few minutes a car or a rattletrap truck pulling farm equipment rumbles over the bridge, or a cloud covers the sun briefly and at least the world changes. After a while Chad speaks.

"Let's bike through Singing Woods. I know a trail that has jumps."

"The one behind the radiator shop?"

"No, a different one. Bigger jumps."

You leave the crayfish and the reflections of the slow water dazzling your eyes and the smell of riverweeds drying on cement, you leave it all behind. Your bikes lay on their sides near the picnic table. There is no one else in the park. You wonder briefly about your parents but the thought has no substance, it doesn't stick. Thoughts are just placeholders, uncanny ghosts poured into forms that appear and disappear.

You get back on your bike and follow Chad over the brown grass of the park. You have decided to set aside the fact that you are not friends, because what else is there. You both set it aside and proceed together haphazardly through the streets and alleys, noticing and then discarding the notice of bottle caps and bits of glass and cans and wrappers and pebbles and the smallest most insignificant things. You hate noticing these cast-off objects. Chad pulls a wheelie for half a block then laughs and you think *he laughs like a burnout* and you envy it, an identity forming in the otherwise hapless Chad. What do you have besides your quiet resentment, your stubborn adolescent work ethic?

A man in a long blue car begins to follow you through the streets. You and Chad turn left, then right, aimlessly, to see if he will follow you. He does. He stays half a block behind but persistently cruises toward you. You can't see his face behind the windshield, except the outline of his sunglasses. He drives ten miles an hour and the steady slowness of his driving disturbs you. It makes you feel spotlit. The sun bakes everything around you into stillness.

"He's following us," Chad says after a while.

You take a shortcut through a parking lot and an alley, and when you arrive back at the street, the blue car is there, turning the corner behind you. A knowledge creeps into your body from the driver's gaze, that this is beyond a game, that the man in the car is a hunter and even though you are both confident you can escape him, being young and on bicycles and at home in the tiny patchwork of streets, this is a new feeling, to be preyed upon and to recognize the sexual outline of your body under his gaze, obscured behind tinted windows as you look over your shoulder laughing at him.

And now the quiet town sits like a crumb on the earth, you see it as if from above. And down in the square of town you see a blue car moving through streets like a toy. A grid has been rolled onto a few miles of land that will bury you, particles carried east, everything in sight eroding downward.

You ride into Singing Woods with Chad to escape the man in the blue car. You were told not to go there and this deepens your urgency. The feeling of flight. You are sure you are justified by your fear. As you wind deeper into the woods you find the trail with rounded humps scattered along its course and you take turns jumping and crashing into saplings on the edge of the path. The blue car and the man's sunglasses have become relics of an abandoned game, shed in favor of the immediate mystery of the bicycle path. The way you can turn anything into a game—this is the form of brilliance that childhood takes. You are just on the edge of losing this brilliance for something else, something oily and desperate that tugs insistently in the night.

You are no longer bored. The blue car man has cured you of boredom. Now you are united and enlivened, riding through the steamy woods in the strangeness of middle day, unaccounted for while the rest of the world did whatever it called work, forever offscreen and thin, unreal. You race in the woods and find a shallow spot in the creek to bike over, legs held up. Chad takes an alternate path and you rejoin at a giant flat rock where you dismount the bikes, then stand on the rock and piss as far as you are both able, manipulating the streams ridiculously and listening to the patter on the leaves and forest floor.

Chad remounts his bicycle and races ahead. He is faster than you, and this bothers you. So for drama, for attention, for revenge, from the desire to create another story or to control the story you are in, you create a tableau. It is probably from a television show, but it is for the game, which remains unnamed, without rules, formless. You lay injured beneath the bike and cry out *help! help!* as if you are trapped. You try to duplicate the reassuring, fake cleanliness of a television accident. Carefully placed. Across the path. One leg trapped beneath the bicycle. You call out again *help! help!* and then listen. You don't hear Chad anywhere and wonder how far up the trail he has gone, how long he will ride until he decides to turn back, how much his pleasure of being ahead of you will be spoiled by the perfect drama of the accident re-creation. The worst thing about Chad, you decide, is that he is unsubtle. That he might not appreciate this twist in the drama at all.

Then at last some far-off movement in the forest, Chad is playing along after all, shuffling through leaves and snapping branches with the kind of lazy footwork you associate with his burnout future. *Help! help!* you call, pretending to be injured, so carefully placed, and Chad moves closer, guided by your cries. He has set his bike down, maybe by the creek or maybe it is broken again; in any case he is in the game. Chad is so careless with his bicycle, his body, his future—almost pridefully so. He smokes cigarettes and hangs out at the mechanic's shop learning to swear.

"Are you alright?" says a man's voice. "What happened." You look up and there on the path is the blue car man, still in his dark glasses. You imagine his car parked and idling at the edge of the woods. You find you are unable to speak. The man steps closer. From your spot on the ground you can see up his t-shirt to his pale, hairy belly. The breast pocket of his T-shirt holds a soft pack of cigarettes. He looks old to you, which means stink and flab and adulthood.

He steps closer and stands over you.

"I'm alright," you manage to say.
The man stares at you.
"I was just kidding."

All around there is the soft twitter of birds. You listen for Chad. Hear the gurgling creek beneath the leaves and birdcall. That's all.

The man frowns. "You shouldn't joke about that," he says, "people will think you're really hurt. I did." He seems angry that you have tricked him. You understand in a quick moment, you reach a new kind of thinking, that somehow he will use this anger as a reason to hurt you, that you are in the wrong and in his mind he has gained an advantage and you are the child who must be punished. You are afraid to stand up because it will move you closer to him. When the man clears his throat you are careful not to show fear, but also afraid that you look like you are trying not to show fear.

The man puts his hand on his hips and looks around, into the forest. You are probably less than a hundred yards from the road but there's no evidence now of a town at all. You might be deep into the Appalachian Trail. You might be in the remote Yukon, where packs of former sled dogs roam feral. You are too quiet to survive here with your small voice. After all no one else heard your bogus cries. He looks down at your shrinking outline. The damp has seeped into all your points of contact with earth. You are a child and he a reeking adult.

The man suddenly hunches and you flinch. You think he means to scare you. His shoulders move up toward his ears and his chest caves in and his hands start up toward his head but they do not make it. His hands become tired on the way to his head, and his knees bend together toward the soft earth, then astonishingly he is on the ground. A large man, flabby and white and still on the forest floor. You have propped yourself onto one arm. Down the path you see Chad staring with his eyes large and his mouth sucked in. The way their two bodies are positioned, the man down on the forest floor and Chad recoiled, one hand moving to his mouth, you understand that Chad has just thrown a rock. That he has somehow, beyond even his own imagining, struck the man's head. It is impossible and the impossible happens every day. The man moves his left fingers weakly, like his disconnected arm is feeling around for its body. Blood on his matted hair. Or did you imagine that. You can hear everything in the woods and everything in the town, and even part of the future, roaring into your mind.

Then you see that Chad has turned to run. And you are on your bicycle without knowing how you picked it up and straddled the seat and began pedaling—that part of your life will forever be a mystery. You only know that you are biking with the strangest certainty of your life, and listening for anything behind you and following Chad as if he were the savior you have heard people sing about outside the closed doors of the tiny Congregational church. And at some point, rounding a curve in this makeshift BMX path in a little patch of woods, you see a clearing, pavement, a driveway. A house bestride the woods and the town. It is the banker's house. Without communicating at all, you both hide your bicycles behind a pile of cut and stacked firewood then crouch there, breathing wildly, listening, every simple sound made strange. Birdcall, squirrel in leaves, hum of electrical wires, far off truckbed bouncing across a gravel road, perhaps a distant maul hitting a spike. The boredom. This time each sound rings with the intensity of survival.

"Do you think he's dead?" you ask.
"You can't kill someone just hitting them with a rock."
"You think he'll follow us?"
"Not in there."

Chad says it nodding at the house. Your eyes widen. Chad peers from behind the woodpile, watching the leaves and tree trunks on the far side of the driveway.

"Listen. I don't think we should."
"I go in people's houses all the time."
"What if it's locked and he sees us?"
"No one locks their doors."

Then you know it will happen, and Chad is not lying about being in people's houses. And at least it's something better than this crouching fear, to ease the side door of the house open, the unlocked summer widening before you, house after house, other people's air conditioning, their refrigerators, their underwear and magazines and lemonade. Chad walks with a practical sudden movement, very calm, in two fast steps toward the cement patio then using one fluid motion he opens the sliding glass door and calls out in a whisper *Hello?* It seems superhuman to you, or alien, extraterrestrial, beyond this life. Chad is inside the house and you are crouched behind the woodpile with the two bicycles, alone, not in any fabricated drama this time, no game whatsoever, just the real crouch of a real and hunted boy.

And then you walk calmly over just as Chad showed you, sure that someone is watching, sure that you have been seen and someone is even now walking up the drive toward you. You lock the sliding glass door behind you and enter the truth of being in a stranger's house, illegally, in the middle of a summer day, the middle of another life. Chad walks toward a doorway and calls again with greater volume *Hello? Is anyone home? Hello?* and with each step forward every little thing in this house takes on the luster of a jewel. The objects speak. Table lamp. Braided rug. Slippers. Last night's newspaper folded to the half-finished crossword. It is like walking inside a mind.

You stop and really look at this container of strange life. It's only this. Places to sit, sleep, eat, watch television, read books. Smell from the residue of bodies safe from the weather and from others. That picture of a gray-haired man praying before a loaf of bread. A Minnesota Vikings tumbler, ice melted to an inch of water at bottom. A deck of cards, slightly askew, atop a maple cribbage board. All the while, the insistent pressing of the blue car man's existence throbs behind you, unknown and invisible, and it will continue to do so in all the years ahead though you will never know him or see him again. This particular force, the fearful and predatory nature of adulthood, will justify dozens of adolescent crimes, in fact this day will form a blueprint. Even though it remains unspoken for most of your life, some idea of the blue car man will press gently at your back in the worst moments. The house hums a steady air-conditioned dream. Chad returns from somewhere holding a can of beer. You realize you've been frozen in place for long minutes, and at his presence your muscles begin to relax. You adjust your breathing to fit the room.

"No one's here. Come on, let's go."
"You think it's safe?"
"Yeah. It's safe."

Chad somehow jams the beer can in the pocket of his cutoff shorts and unlocks the sliding glass door. One foot out. Another. He looks around, one hand still tethered to the safety of the house. You follow him in the kind of faithful awe reserved for accomplices. The stinging pressure of sunlight returns to the tops of your arms and legs and forehead. You ride your bicycle right out the driveway, up to the corner, and just like that you're four blocks from home.

"What are you going to do with the beer?"
"Hide it."
"I want some."
"You should have taken one then."
Shrug.

The bright sudden day has become late afternoon; the sounds of people have grown weary and rounded. Part of you listens for cars as you sit in the street, twirling your handlebars. Part of you somewhere is just normal though that part has temporarily flown off and hovers nearby. You nod to Chad as if to say you are done, but over your right shoulder you see an unusual movement and your insides jump. The tiny head appears, followed by the enormous body, of a wild turkey. Then another. Four of them, mammoth and gaited like shrunken giants, walk out of the woods and onto the road. Chad waves and bikes off, beer can wedged into his pocket, yelling the perfect burnout *Adios* over his shoulder. The birds are as tall as your bicycle, and they scare you. You ride away from them alone, quickly as possible, hesitating at each intersection and watching closely for blue cars, then biking ridiculously through, legs pumping wildly. Anyone would think you are a kid in an imaginary race, a lonely game.

I wanted to tell you. You look back now at the summer, the ridge in the green dusk, the old stagecoach road, the abandoned brewery, the parking lot nearby, the saplings, the creek, the bleeding man face down on the path, and it forms a map, the first map, because maps are made to navigate danger, to make each other aware of danger, to abstract it, shape it, make it familiar. In this first map, the woods are now a tiny patch of trees along an unfarmable limestone ridge near a small creek. They are surrounded by fields and farms and farm towns and predators and lonely old men who drive slowly through the streets wearing sunglasses, never speaking, like the hands of a clock. What moves across a face is time. You wouldn't recognize Chad if you saw him today. He has disappeared. The man who drove the blue car has disappeared. Yet on the first map, there exists a small red stain on the path near the creek where he has spoken the words and now lies face down, captured by time and by cartography.

He may have been there to help you. He may have been a demon. On the first map there is always a border where the known and the unknown meet. The map says begin *here*; your knowledge ends *there*. The man face down, bleeding from his head, and Chad running for his bike. And you are frozen for a moment. The day is glass and you are almost a real boy.

When you return home everything waits as you left it. The grass and the empty yard are finally your friend. You walk into sunlight. It is your sunlight. A red rubber kickball. The neighbor's dog on his chain. The dog is your friend. The impossibly large oak tree. Stand back from the acetylene torch. Stand back from the car. Stay out of the road. It is your plate of cookies. It is your purple shirt on the clothesline and it is finally your friend. The rosebush and decaying garage. Smell of oil soaking into concrete. Uncomfortable friend. Stay back from the lawnmower. From the oven. Wind moans through leaves. Sound and light are finally your friend. No one is there. The feeling of summer. The empty house. No one is there.

# THE TWO DAUGHTERS

AT THAT TIME I lived on the edge of town in a small house by Singing Woods with my two daughters, who were always hungry. I never seemed to have enough food for them. They were growing into young women who ate more and more and sometimes they stood in front of the open cupboard doors, peering in and growling. Their shoulder blades stuck out. I shopped and I gardened and I cooked but there was not enough. Eventually they took to hunting in Singing Woods while I was away at work. Imagine my surprise to come home and find a dead rabbit hanging from our clothesline, blood gathered on the grass. What was happening to my daughters?

When asked, first one then the other replied simply, "We were hungry." Then they would shrug or turn on the TV or sulk in their bedroom. I watched the way they looked at each other, as if gauging how far the other had given in to a force from beyond the horizon, each daring the other to go further.

It was summer and school was out. Sometimes they didn't go to school anyway, my feral daughters. But in summer their boredom often escalated into rage and their bedroom turned brutish, swamp-like, musty. I was glad they managed not to hurt each other.

The oldest liked to dig little graves and bury effigies. The youngest liked to spy on the people and animals up and down our road. I suspected they might not be popular at school.

One night I was awakened by the sound of a window creaking open. I got out of bed and walked in the quiet, dark house, stepping cautiously through the gray hall. I looked in their bedroom—empty. Out the window I saw my hungry daughters disappearing into Singing Woods. I called their names but they didn't turn around. I didn't know what to do. The night felt strangely oversized—a giant night. I could hear tree frogs gathering strength in unison.

I took a flashlight from the basement and shined it toward the trees but its light only emphasized the darkness all around. I walked into the woods. I could not hear them. I called their names and wandered until I was afraid I might get lost. Occasionally I heard moving animal sounds but darkness amplified every little noise. Eventually I found myself facing our house again, convinced that my daughters would return any minute, and I went inside and turned on all the lights. I began cleaning. There seemed no other way to wait. After cleaning each room, I turned off its light. Room by room, the house was extinguished.

I waited.

Finally my hungry daughters returned. Their faces were different—painted in dazzling colors. I watched them climb back through the window, out of the dark blue morning and into their little box of bedroom. I surprised them by turning on the light.

"Father!" said the oldest daughter.

"Turn off the light," said the youngest, squinting.

"Where have you been?" I asked.

The two girls, tired and ragged, sank down into their beds.

"We haven't been anywhere," said the oldest, and the youngest nodded. I noticed some scratches and bruises on their long, wild limbs. I could see them deciding what to tell. They looked at each other and came to unspoken agreement, my telepathic daughters.

"We visit the bears," said the older daughter. "There's an old bear who lives in the forest and she has two sons."

"We like them," said the youngest, slowly. Her eyes were already closed. I became worried about them falling asleep, as if they had concussions.

"You must not visit the bears," I said. "And you must not paint on your faces." The girls were already drifting.

"But we look like fantastic goddesses," said the younger.

I watched them ease into exhausted sleep and soon enough morning light entered the room. At breakfast they looked like my two daughters again, young and pale and hungry, though their hunger had begun to grow a tendril.

———————

The next night before bed I sat down next to my daughters, their room lit pink by a bedside lamp, their faces sleepy and hungry and flush. I said, "I would like to tell you a story."

"Yes," they said, sleepily and hungrily. "Sure."

"I would like to tell you the story of the bears."

That got their attention. They each shifted to face me and opened their eyes, the oldest propped on her elbows.

"Once upon a time there was a family, much like our family, except the opposite. Instead of a father and two daughters there was a mother and two sons. And the sons grew up playing in Singing Woods."

"What happened to the father?" my youngest daughter said.

"He was accidentally shot," I told her. "By a hunter."

"This is a scary story," said my oldest daughter.

"One day the two boys found an abandoned hut in the woods and decided to make it their second, secret home. But whenever they entered the hut, they felt funny."

"Funny how?" asked the younger.

"Like they wanted to fight each other, and they became very itchy, and their tongues hung out of their mouths and they could smell strange smells from far away. They could smell bees and grasshoppers and mushrooms all across the forest."

"Cool," said the older.

"They had stumbled on a witch's hut. In the day, she lived in town. She was a schoolteacher."

My daughters gave each other knowing looks. Of course their teachers were witches.

But at night she often came to the hut in the woods. And there was a spell on the hut. It had a way of turning people into animals."

Outside the night was full with stars and a waning quarter moon sat in the silver maple leaves as they flashed their undersides in the wind. The night became part of the story.

I told them, "One day the boys went to the hut and started fighting. They even bit each other; they couldn't help themselves. And they didn't notice darkness had come. They decided to stay in the hut instead of risking the forest at night. But then the witch appeared, of course."

"What did she do?" said one.

"How did she get there? Don't say on a broom," said the other.

"The witch rode in on a giant black bear. The two boys were terrified, but they asked her for help. The witch said 'You've broken into my home and made a mess of it. I can smell that you have good livers, which I like. I think I will have my friend rip out your insides so I can use them.'

"'No, no, please,' the boys begged. And the witch considered. She said 'I'll give you a choice. You can become bears and do my bidding, or you can become ingredients.'

"Of course the boys submitted to the witch's magic and were turned into bears. Those are the two bears you meet in the woods. They are not to be trusted. They kill young girls and bring their livers to the witch if she tells them to."

"But what about the mother?" asked the older. "You said there was a mother."

"Well, don't you think a mother would go looking for her sons? And recognize their torn clothes in the hut? And wait for them there?"

They nodded.

"And given the choice by the witch to be with her sons as a mother bear or never see them again, which do you think she would choose?"

The girls sank down under their covers. "Mother bear," the youngest said.

"Please don't sneak out into the woods," I asked of them.

"Would you become a bear for us?" asked the older, her eyes narrow.

"Please," I said. "Sleep."

———————

The next morning I awoke and a strange light had entered the house. I was alone—the girls had gone out again. I was perhaps much older.

I walked outside. Dawn light shone silver in the yard. I saw my two daughters standing at the edge of the woods. It was as close as they would come to the house. I called to them and the youngest took half a step back. Her legs were painted white. I held up my hands, imploring them not to leave.

Everything wild will appear as it is, only that.

How many mornings had I been coaxing them back to the house? I went back inside and searched their bedroom for their school thermoses. I filled them with lemonade.

Outside the birds had grown noisy. I waited in the grainy light with the two thermoses of lemonade.

Then the eldest stepped from the woods. I rolled the thermoses toward her and she picked them up.

I thought perhaps this meant I was still her father.

Behind them in the woods I saw flashes of fur. The girls turned and ran. What had I done to startle them?

I was sure they had gone feral in the woods. I stood in the yard and felt the pain of it in my skin. It would be impossible to lie in a bed now. Each position would be like the edge of a knife on my body, because they were gone from me. I thought perhaps I should buy a camera with a powerful lens and try to take their pictures. My heart had fallen out. I imagined a day when they no longer came to the house, no longer even recognized it. When they were simply gone, wild, fallen out of the habit of civilization.

I wasn't sure what was a dream and what was a thought and what was my daily life. I knew my daughters' legs were painted white. I knew there was a pitcher of lemonade in the refrigerator. I knew their bedroom was empty.

I had a vision of my oldest daughter singing to a bear and the bear burst into tears. It was not quite like dreaming.

———

At sunrise my two daughters returned from hunting in the woods, carrying the carcass of a young bear. Its legs were bound together over a long, sagging branch and the girls struggled with the weight, eldest daughter at the front, youngest behind. They seemed superhuman.

Are my daughters the type of girls who roast and eat their boyfriends?

They lowered the dead bear to the grass of the back lawn, clouds turning pink over them with the rising sun. They untied the bear's legs.

"We stole him from the witch," the youngest said.

"And killed him," said the oldest over her shoulder. They walked off, into the garage.

A clear patch of sky to the west brought its good fortune to us. One star still hung there. And one star in the mouth of the bear. And a star in each of my daughters.

What star spun inside me? I could remember once rocking each daughter in my arms. How for each of them I had a little song.

The oldest returned with a saw.

The youngest with a shovel.

I was like a distant planet. Perhaps Neptune.

"We'll cut up our new boyfriend," said the oldest, "and remake the world."

# HOW I BECAME A MOTHER

I WAS THERE when she uncovered the baby and I saw that it had no head. It was my first morning; it was my first time. I saw the stump coming out of the baby's shoulders and even though I was prepared for it I felt great shock and a wave of nausea, and I sat down. I had always believed the fates were blue and blissful and healing people all the time despite their sharp teeth but the thought of the headless baby going to heaven deeply freaked me out.

She said her name was Katherine the Great. We sat together for a while then she stood up and took the headless baby out the back door. She was gone for about fifteen minutes. While I waited I tried not to see the headless baby in my mind. I imagined a large floating bubble and inside it a wonderful aisle of products but when I reached for the first item on the shelf I held in my hands the headless baby. I got up and rummaged in the cupboards. I was afraid of the windows. The cupboards swirled with paint that seemed to portray a never-ending wind. It was a small dark house, one floor and three rooms. I found a bottle and a glass and while I waited I drank a little vodka, even though it was morning.

I must have come from somewhere. I may have been in a house or just a head, a dream. The night before, drunk, I had fallen into the ravine behind the Wal-Mart parking lot. In shipping and receiving, sometimes we party. I was a mess. I lay in the bottom of the ravine crying out and I heard her voice.

She had been walking the baby around to get it to stop crying. There was a larger crying happening too, not in sound waves but in stillness, as if coming through our bodies from all over earth. She said she would put the baby down and get a rope. I remember watching the stars and touching my body to see who I was and what was bleeding. I sat in the rocks and weeds and waited. I must have hit my head—I was nauseous and out of balance. I moaned and called out, above the larger crying, so she could find me again.

She simply came back and threw down a rope. I thought of children eating supper, learning their letters everywhere, eating dirt. I thought *maybe she is a constellation and I am going up to the heavens.* The woman's eyes bulged out and she wore her coarse hair pulled back. She was surrounded by a purple death cloud, difficult to see though certainly the aura could be known.

All that was last night. Now she returned without the headless baby and we sat in silence. Then she got up to make tea. I asked her what she did with the baby.

"I put it in the cave."
"What cave?"
"The cave of my dead babies."

I asked about the father, and she told me she had gotten pregnant from eating an egg with a spell on it. She said, "Every night since, I have given birth to a baby and every morning I wake to find its head has been cut off." We waited for the tea. I felt made of cobwebs and I didn't know if I was normal. I could hear traffic from outside, and the room gradually brightened. "The head disappears," she said. "It becomes unknown. No person or thing will bring back the head."

"Well, there must be demons somewhere," I said.

"There are a lot of demons. They crawl out of the pipes behind Wal-Mart all the time."

I felt uncomfortable. I wondered if I had been pulled into the ravine by a demon. I wondered if I myself was inhabited by a demon, and if she might be seeking revenge. Would I know if I had become a demon?

The woman rubbed her hands across the low part of her belly. "Feel it," she commanded. "I think there's another baby coming already." I put my hand on her belly. I couldn't tell.

When I took my hand back it was warm and I thought *what if my hand turned to a warm stone that ringed a campfire?* I still wasn't right. Tea was ready and we sat together, deeper and deeper into silence. We seemed miles from circuitry and art galleries and even further from the news reports of gouged out eyes and bombing victims all across the globe. We went as far inward as a skyscraper goes up, just having our tea in golden light.

She told me, "The demons are mostly fathers. They tear the birds off trees and brush them around everywhere like they are writing something. Then what's left but an egg full of bad magic. But some of the demons are alien bacteria too. Some of them are just spectral vaginas that spit out names of products. Birth is really fucked up here in Singing Woods."

As we sat taking tea the day grew warmer and I noticed her belly had swollen a little. Of course I wanted to stay for the birth, and I didn't have to work until the next evening. I believed I had stumbled into some kind of psychedelic experiment.

I noticed the sun causing pain in my body; it was worse near the windows. I was full of scrapes and bruises and bad flashes of dream. Katherine said, "You need a lie down. You've had a nasty fall." Outside birds whipped past the windows and crows called from high in the trees.

I stretched out on her bed. "Tell me more about the babies," I said. Katherine smoothed her death cloud. "They are all boys," she said, "and they all die. All I know is that now I produce them." I crossed my hands over my chest, closed my eyes, and fell almost immediately into ultraviolet light. As I fell Katherine said, "Don't turn into fog," and she laughed.

When I woke, Katherine was delivering another baby—crowning, crowning, crowning. The baby slid out with a wonderful sound. I got up and held the dripping baby upside down, cord still connected, and scooped its mouth free of mucus. We worked together and I took her instruction; she had done this many times. The fading daylight was nothing compared to the light from the baby.

Katherine was exhausted. I finished cleaning the baby then placed him in her arms. Everything was normal and the baby, struggling to live, made me forget about the curse. I excused myself and walked back to the ravine. Through the trees I could see a truck at the loading dock and the driver writing something on a clipboard. I gently pitched the cord and the afterbirth into the ravine and asked for the child to be blessed.

Back at the house she said, "Everything happens fast here in Singing Woods." Were we a family now? She sat recovering with her darling boy. It seemed heaven boiled wherever a child landed.

Family work at first meant just staring at the baby. Then it changed. I went outside and listened to the wind and birds. I walked back to the ravine and again I looked across at the Wal-Mart loading dock. I thought I might have been inside some display, but it seemed no one saw us. Singing Woods seemed a forgotten place.

When I returned, Katherine had changed her clothing. I couldn't see her death cloud. The baby lay swaddled on the bed. She said playfully to me, "I know—let's try a game. You be the mother and I'll be the no-good. We'll change places." I didn't know what to say. She handed me the baby and got the vodka down from the cupboard. I tried to think of myself as a mother. The baby shook with little whimpers. I sat and rocked him. I liked this game—I felt like I could be king and queen at once.

Evening deepened and demons slid from the pipes behind Wal-mart. For a while we chatted about made up things like the stock market and politics and daydreams. Then Katherine went out to get more liquor. I tried to stay awake. I felt heroic for trying, but somewhere in the night I must have dozed off and gotten entangled with my ultraviolet self from dreams. When I woke, I looked to my lap and saw the baby, pudgy and stiff and headless. Katherine was gone. I called her name three times. Where the baby's head was supposed to be, there was just a bloody stump, exactly as before. It was my first baby; it was my first time as mother.

I sat and cried until I had nothing left. The baby had grown stiff; I put it in a bed of towels in the kitchen sink. I thought about curses—how a curse is not undone by reversing the actions of its placement, because a curse is not symmetrical. I looked around the room and noticed how a curse affected objects as well as people. How neither paying more attention nor less attention to your curse brings relief. Certainly the cure for a curse involved sacrifice, supplication, pain and illness. I missed my baby. Our universe might be a cursed universe. In fact, a curse might be a superior life form; it might be spiritual, intelligent, magical. These thoughts did not comfort me, and Katherine did not come back.

I went out to find the cave. The morning was smaller than yesterday's morning, and redder. I followed a trail up a small ridge. To my far right I could see across the ravine, to the loading docks behind Wal-Mart and beyond, to the county road that led into town. I could see demon shapes in the ravine, and imagined I could see old umbilical cords. To my left the jagged limestone cliffs stretched to a second ridge. I realized I had started my new life as a producer—each evening the pregnancy and each morning the headless baby.

At the end of the path I fumbled along a limestone wall, carrying the stiff, headless baby in a bundle of blankets until I reached a cave. I couldn't look inside. I tossed the dead baby in, saying *forgive me,* and there was no sound of landing, as if the baby had disappeared after crossing the cave threshold. Or perhaps it floated.

After that morning, I settled in. It's strange what becomes normal. In my new life as the producer behind Wal-Mart I was mostly invisible. I developed a peculiar belief—that a father consumer who rose from a sea of milk would give me purpose, and the phantoms that waned and disappeared in the gloomy caverns behind Wal-mart would befriend me. We were all passengers in a mirage of distortion. Perhaps the magic egg was more like an idea, a thought. Or worse, a psychic blind spot. In any case I would have the solitary life of motherhood and martyrdom, like a pair of blind twin dolls.

Katherine had escaped across a border I didn't even know about yet. On the walk back that first day, I imagined a cave full of floating decapitated babies. Probably the cave was another womb, and I was throwing the babies to their future in another system. I had worked on assembly lines before. I wanted to believe I was helping someone.

I try to pay attention. Some nights ago I dreamt I was inside the egg. I was the curse, but I was also just me, my body. A hazy light came through the egg and I began to feel the shadows of leaves blocking the sunlight. There was a rhythm to it, and I could hear the world outside the egg but I could not be a part of it. Maybe the curse was just separation. Sometimes I think the little house in the woods is the egg, and I might never be strong enough to leave it. Or I might need help, just like Katherine the Great.

The reason I'm telling all this is that now we should switch places. Any way you like. You be the pregnancy and I'll be the headless baby. Or you be the demon and I'll be the woman with a rope. You be the egg and I'll be an empty house in the woods behind Wal-Mart. You be a bird, and I'll be a curse, brushing you around in the air, writing you this demon letter.

# THE STORY OF THE BOX

GRANDFATHER SAT ASLEEP again in the bright day, in the quiet house. Cee Cee wandered the rooms, restless as a flame. Then out to the back yard where she heard manic rustling from the edge of the forest, as if from some being in trouble, and set off to investigate. The yard edged a patch of woods that quieted the encroaching developments, a wild strip that led to the larger woods beyond.

Cee Cee walked toward the sound and it stopped; she stood still and waited.

Each time the rustling started, she stepped closer until it stopped. An animal was struggling, she was sure of that. She felt drawn to a spot of intensity in the yard. Gradually, she stepped closer and closer. Her breathing slowed; she crouched. Then she saw the squirrel, too young to be alone, its little mouth open and its chest heaving.

She bent over it and murmured some words from church mixed with some words from Grandmother. The squirrel was sick too. She made a nest of leaves in her hand and picked up the warm, light body. It seemed to be in shock. She carried it across the yard and into the house, carefully sliding the screen door open while holding the squirrel close and level.

She put the squirrel in a shoebox and placed it on the footstool, then covered it with a washcloth. Its breath came slow and it blinked every so often. When she stroked its back, it gasped and tried to swallow.

Grandfather said, "What are you doing with that, and how did it get so small?"

"I think it's going to die," she said.

Grandfather stared, his veins like blue paper pasted to his skin. She could not tell how he was seeing, through what material or memory. He asked her how old she was. "I'm almost nine," she said. He watched something moving through the air behind her, but when she turned around there was nothing. So she helped him with the television remote and brought him a glass of water.

Eventually when they checked on the squirrel, it was dead.

Grandfather said, "Bring me my pocketknife."

She went to his dresser, where he kept his pocket change and handkerchief and keys and a small, folding knife. The house clicked and whirred with systems of heating and cooling and, it seemed, breathing. It went on without them. Outside shadows showed how summer wind whipped the new leaves.

She handed him the knife. His fingers seemed too large and numb to open it but when she reached to help him, he grew angry. He fumbled on. Eventually the little blade clicked into place. The house clicked on too.

Grandfather looked at the inside of the tiny squirrel, cutting and then prying the ribs apart with two fingers. He said, "If you want me to live, you have to kill one of each of the animals in the forest. They all have a little section of my heart." The oxygen tank wheezed. He stared over his glasses at her.

She thought for a second that he was dreaming, but that didn't explain her part in the situation. It was puzzling.

He handed her the torn apart squirrel, still warm, and said, "Get rid of this."

Then she was just a girl holding a shoebox in a suburban house, like anyone, anywhere.

She believed it was right to listen to grandfather, but she also believed it was wrong to kill the animals. She felt as if a light had come over them there in the living room and inside that circle of light she had entered grandfather's dream, with its strange rules.

She said, "Yes sir," and even bowed slightly, then walked out of the living room and to the back door. She had never called him sir before. She thought it would be right to keep grandfather alive as long as possible, as she walked in the backyard kicking a rock along. Where the forest started now there seemed an impenetrable darkness and each bright bird sang its unseen life to her. What dreams did she have to tend, she wondered.

———————

Cee Cee watched Grandfather dim and brighten in a wavelike pattern. She heard snoring above the slow pulse of the oxygen tank and finally snuck upstairs to the locked hall closet, where she brought the box down from the top shelf and took out the smaller key hanging on a little nail inside the closet. She opened the box.

She had been told never to open the box. Inside she found an 'oral syringe' and a set of instructions. She read all the words and looked at the terrible charts. Then she sat down in the hallway and wondered about her family. About Grandfather, of course, but also her aunts and uncles. She was the youngest. They still called her *baby girl*. They said she had it easy.

She locked the box, placed it carefully back on the top shelf and locked the closet. She could hear the furnace, the grandfather clock, the oxygen tank and the snoring. The occasional bird from outside. She smelled the hot dusty odor of the wooden shelves.

Back downstairs she looked at Grandfather, his cruel lips and fluttering eyelids. The skin of his hand grown sheer like a nightgown or curtain and all the poison blood going around and around, a horrible diseased carousel: Grandfather the grotesque carousel pony. Grandfather the box of poison. Grandfather the rung bell. Grandfather the dead strand of hair.

She stood over him with her difficult feeling. Maybe it was like a broadening, maybe an opening up, but also maybe a hardening scar. Maybe a tingling through her body where tragic knowledge could root. Outside birds skittered among the leaves; they seemed sinister. More light would arrive soon, earth kept turning around. She felt focused as a lens, all the wild feelings named Grandfather suddenly one, and what a fool she had been. The mountain was finally only a mountain, the silence deeper because it attached to other silences and inside them she was small and alone, making her choices in the world.

Then Grandfather woke up.

She said, "Grandfather, I looked in the box."

"You what?" He was confused; he didn't know what she was talking about. He struggled to say something and gestured weakly with his right hand. After a moment he fell back asleep.

At that moment she wanted everyone to know she looked in the box. She wanted everyone to know about the box in the closet and the person inside each of us waiting to use it. She wanted to understand this difficult feeling.

———————

By late afternoon the heat of the yard and the suffocating hush of the house had grown unbearable.

She stepped into the cool forest and caught her sweatshirt on a wild raspberry bush. When she turned around she saw the house and the flickering blue television light filling the living room window in mechanical rhythm. She could imagine grandfather there, tracking her. The house looked monstrous.

She walked further into the woods and it seemed there were only two choices: kill the animals or kill Grandfather. She wondered why a grandchild would have to make this choice.

The sun hung low through the treeline until the tree trunks and the space around them turned dark blue, then gray. She found a deer path and followed it for a while, then stopped and listened. All around she heard rustling in leaves, wings flapping, toads and birds and crickets calling out. They spoke to her but not only to her. Everyone spoke to everyone in the woods.

Then she heard Grandmother, calling her name and shouting "dinner's ready," and she turned back toward the lights of the house.

———————

Grandfather ate in his chair and demanded various attentions. Grandmother busied herself, eating a little then standing back up to check a dish or a thermostat, her hair immovable and auburn, a brittle helmet.

The strangeness of mashed potatoes in summer.

They had entered limbo. They ate quietly and felt heartbreak. Grandfather said, "I need more butter," but on his plate there was nothing left to smear with butter. Grandmother passed it to him. He just needed it.

After dinner, Cee Cee's thoughts began to tumble. Grandmother loaded the dishwasher while Cee Cee played solitaire on the living room floor. On the television screen, bodies were being ripped apart by bullets and dissected by doctors and punched in the face and tied to chairs. All the night was one long assault against the body set to strange, pulsing music. Occasionally Grandfather laughed.

Grandmother read in her chair, feet up. Grandfather dozed in and out, in and out, his reality like a breath. Cee Cee lay her face on the cool plastic of the playing cards. Together they all eased into drifting night.

Cee Cee woke and needed to go to the bathroom; she sat up with the six of diamonds stuck to her face. The house had changed shape, and parts of it were inside out. Parts of it were forest now.

Grandfather said, "I will make my dream smaller and smaller so you can find everything."

He stood outside the bathroom door. A fluttering giant.

She woke again and walked out the side door to the edge of the yard and the seething trees. The giant metal box of the air conditioner hummed to her left. She walked straight ahead, toward the dark recesses of woods edge.

All was dream. She had learned that in school, minute by minute. At the grassy edge, where the lawnmower could no longer encroach, she knelt and watched. Her eyes adjusted to the dream.

The first animal arrived, unhurried, poking its nose here and there. In strange moonlight she saw a path, and the animal turned to look at her directly before walking away down the path. She didn't know if it had called to her or dared her. She had forgotten a lot of words and her mouth ached.

Dream Grandfather said, "Let us embrace our fragility as we await merciful absorption." He stood watching from the doorway. Again he loomed. He wavered in and out of his form.

Cee Cee stood and pointed. She called him to the path in the woods but he shook his head no. His dream ended at the patio door. "I suffer this *distinguishment*," he said, which meant what?

Once Grandfather had told her, "In all the stories in which one action is forbidden, that action *must* be taken. Someone looks back, someone else turns into salt. Someone gives out a key and someone else unlocks the door to a bloody room full of bodies. Someone demands that a specific jar not be opened, and someone else releases a plague of evil. Get it?" And she remembered this, and she remembered the feel of it—bright pink.

She woke again. She had almost peed. She stood and hurried down the hall.

———

In her forays she had so far identified seven non-bird animals in their patch of Singing Woods: Deer, squirrel, fox, mouse, rabbit, chipmunk, and raccoon. There were too many birds to list. Owl, blue jay, robin, sparrow, grackle, crow, chickadee, hawk, woodpecker… she went dizzy with them.

She decided to collect hearts from each of the seven animals she knew of and leave the birds alone. Grandfather specifically needed their hearts; his own heart was failing. That seemed logical.

She didn't know what he would do with them. She didn't know how to trap a fox. She thought she could catch a mouse and a chipmunk easily enough, though.

One by one she would bring the hearts to Grandfather, still beating. And then what. She imagined a shoebox. The chipmunk on its back, neatly slit open and still breathing in a nest of leaves and grass, presented like a fancy lunch plate.

"Here, Grandfather, is the still beating heart of a chipmunk. Will this save you?"

She imaged Grandfather brightening from his stupor, saying, "No, granddaughter, you still have five hearts to go." Then he would rip the little heart from the body and eat it. He would become stronger and send her back to the woods.

She imagined many more conversations with Grandfather than were ever spoken aloud. All her life this had been the case.

She thought *how would I bring him a deer?* and pictured Grandfather with his oxygen tank and half-closed eyes. And felt again that he might be a demon.

—————

Deep into the morning, she lay asleep and warm with a feeling of being surrounded by rain—but invisible, a mind rain, a billowy curtain. The blanket as heavy as a continent, and her eyelids little continents too, her eyelids basically Australia. She pondered this cosmic feeling, mouth open.

She heard a crashing noise.

She got up from bed and walked downstairs toward the flickering living room. The television was still on. The oxygen tank hummed and clicked.

On the screen she saw the heart of a deer. As she watched it beating, her own heart synched up with the dear's heart on television and the oxygen tank. Grandfather was gone. She followed the lines of oxygen; they were connected to the television. Maybe Grandfather had been replaced by the deer's heart, pulled from its body and presented on a velvet cloth on television, oxygen tubes entering its meat.

She began to search for Grandfather. Empty kitchen. Empty dining room. She heard a noise in the living room, again the manic rustling sound. She hesitated; the living room was dark and there was a smell. Fear now pulsed with the rhythm of the heart and the tank.

She turned on the light. The deer raised its head. There it was.

The deer stood by the piano, chest cavity opened and dripping blood but alive and shining. She was eating.

Cee Cee moved around the armchair and saw grandfather's feet, sticking out from where the deer had been grazing. Blood around the deer's muzzle.

Then its neck arched unnaturally and it stepped backward as if propelled by a force from inside. The deer was choking. A terrible sound issued into the room, a wet, deep unclogging, then Grandfather's heart slid out of the deer's throat onto the carpet.

———————

In the morning, Grandfather's body had grown further slack, though his breathing marched on. A new smell arose in the room, like decaying band-aids. Grandmother stood over him. She petted his arm like it was a housecat and seemed on the verge of tears. His breath cycled on without care. She leaned to his ear and kept her voice low as if telling a secret. No part of him responded.

Then she turned to Cee Cee. "You stay here with him for just an hour," she said. "I'm going to church. He needs prayers."

The television was still torturing bodies but no sound came from them. Grandmother took her keys from the hook and went to the garage, holding a tissue to her face. Cee Cee watched her car leave the driveway from a front window. Then she went upstairs, to the closet. She removed the box and carefully re-read the instructions. There were two different types of medicine, according to purpose.

In this case, all the medicine was to be taken at once. The subject should be restrained from vomiting, if possible. Because the body tries.

She pocketed the medicine and syringe, then found a shoebox in the lower regions of the closet. Down the stairs and to the ragged edge of Singing Woods. Time was doing something strange; it stopped and sped up at the same instant. It telescoped. She fashioned a little nest in the shoebox with leaves and sticks and looked around. Nothing moved.

Back inside she brought a glass of water to Grandfather's tray then retreated. She prepared the oral syringe just as she had seen in the instructions and on the television. She approached again, Grandfather's body clicking and wheezing there before his lord.

"Grandfather." His breathing did not register her voice. "Grandfather, I have the heart of a rabbit here. You need to eat it. It will make you strong. Grandfather."

She touched his face and in reflex he opened his mouth a little. She pulled his jaw down just enough and slipped the syringe between his teeth. Then closed his mouth firmly with her hand. He tried to gag but he was weak. She didn't let him.

She stroked his throat and waited for him to swallow, just as she had seen her cousin do when she gave medicine to the dog.

Grandfather swallowed. She wiped her wet hands on the rug. A squirrel hung from a branch outside the window, trying to get at the bird feeder. She watched TV while she waited.

---

Slowly she removed the oxygen tube from Grandfather's nose and passed it over his head, where it haloed the tenderness of his flesh. There was no sound from his body, no wave of being. Next, she tried to drag him down the hall by the ankles. She pulled him from the chair and tried not to think. He landed heavily on his back. She tried to think only of love. His body was the heaviest thing she'd ever moved and she couldn't move it far. Eventually, though she found she was weeping, she located the old skateboard in the foul, musty garage and maneuvered it under his spine.

She wondered if she had fallen in love with death.

When she opened the sliding door birds called from all across the back yard and the forest. She dragged Grandfather out into the birdsong, heartless, in his pajamas. His eyes, peaceful and flat, reflected the blue above.

She arranged grandfather in the middle of the back yard and waited.

After what seemed a long time a bold fat robin landed close to her and she sat still as possible, a few feet from Grandfather. They watched each other.

When more birds came, she would go back into the house and turn off the television.

And she knew they would come.

Grandfather, the heartless shrine.

The robin hopped near Grandfather's leg and cocked one eye. It hopped to Grandfather's shoe. His dying smell must have sent a torrent of love into the yard. A few bees began to arrive near the head. She listened.

Everyone would have such pity for her. How she had tried to save him. Larger birds circled above. She could just make out the path in the woods and imagined the animals waiting there. Grandfather twitched, or was it already the tug of a beast upon his flesh.

# THE WEEPER

## WORK

The campus sat near a suburban thruway Northwest of the city, abutting a large forest and a small river, and it required an early start. I had never heard of the school—The Northwest Academy of Arts and Social Sciences—but had received the usual morning phone call requesting a substitute teacher. I accepted.

On the phone, Renata, the coordinator, said, "It's just for one class." Renata had once been a teacher, as well as a message therapist and a standardized test scorer. She moved here because of a divorce, like me, and she told me she had resolved to live simply, without drama. I believed her. She was also my pot dealer, and the connection for most of the other subs, which was handy. She had a subtle way of showing you that you made everything too complicated.

"What is the class?"
"Social Arts."
"I'm not licensed in that."
"No one is. You'll be fine. Take attendance, be firm but kind, follow the lesson plan."

Whenever I expressed doubt, Renata said exactly that, without irony.

The drive from the east side would take nearly 40 minutes. I calculated the gas in my tank and found last night's money folded in a dress pocket. I grabbed the book I was reading and an orange. Simple.

I was licensed for 5-12 social studies, provisionally, while I waited for my equivalency application to be approved. I'd been licensed in a neighboring state and just moved to this new and underwhelming city. Or town, really. After the divorce.

As I drove, I smiled broadly. This was my practice. I didn't want to be another dead-faced driver. Faces in cars could seem dead. If I was smiling, I might catch someone by surprise, and they might smile too.

In the early mornings of this new place diesel pickup trucks moved slowly along the county highways and might appear suddenly after a small rise. I stayed alert as I watched the neighborhoods, the suburbs, the scrubland pass by. I gained in elevation and watched for crows, hawks, vultures, children. I kept the radio off. The farmland ended.

After I left the main road, faded Northwest Academy signs appeared amongst the pines. Finally, I turned up a gravel drive to the large and somewhat dilapidated campus. Students had strung hammocks between the ragged pine trees, and I saw by the bright sagging bellies of synthetic fabric that a few of them were occupied.

I sat in my car in the parking lot. From my tumultuous marriage I had learned to treasure moments of peace. I watched a sparrow moving nearer and nearer the car, pecking at sand. I saw time escaping from its little body. I checked my teeth; I checked my cleavage. I breathed all the way out and held my empty lungs still for a count of three.

The main entrance to The Northwest Academy of Arts and Social Sciences presented a beautiful copper façade, shining over its ruinous details. I walked in and smelled the smell. A school introduces its history to you via scent. This one reminded me of Renata's little house—window cleaner, marijuana, boiled pasta, sharpies, new furniture, old shoes. I walked up to a counter, behind which a dull florescent office hummed in the lunchtime daze.

"I'm here for social arts," I said, and a short, fit woman with dyed black hair set a clipboard on the counter separating us.

"First time here, right?" She handed me a red nametag sticker that read, "visitor."

"What should I know?"

"The less you know, the better," she said, and handed me a sheet of names.

"Is there a lesson plan?"

"They'll know what to do. Stay out of their way. You're in East 202." She pointed out the door and to the left. "Other side of the athletic field, past the volleyball court."

It was only one class.

The school had once been something else. A compound. A set of offices. A seminary? I could feel it, but I couldn't think it through.

I walked past a fountain, dry of water and completely covered in benign graffiti. One scrawl read *freedom to move in all worlds*. I saw an old-fashioned bicycle balanced high up in one of the pine trees.

East Building seemed relatively deserted. I met a member of the maintenance staff, a blonde woman in jeans carrying a portable drill. She walked slowly through the main floor hallway, looking up at the plaster ceiling.

I stopped and stood next to her, looking up also. The ceiling had been patched in places, but also painted—intricate designs painted white on white, just noticeable.

"How did they do that?" I asked. The maintenance worker ignored me. She squeezed the trigger on the portable drill which engaged and made a brief sound, a sort of general-purpose answer. *She loves that sound*, I thought.

"Where is 202?"

"It's upstairs, all the way down," she said, smiling, still looking at the ceiling.

"Where are all the students?"

"Waiting. Working. Sleeping." She shrugged, then squeezed the trigger once quickly to indicate that our conversation was over.

My husband had been an artist. Brilliant in his way, unstable and visionary, at the mercy of his cruel upbringing and its required exorcism. He photographed the poignant detritus of family life and enlarged the photos to make sets for inscrutable yet moving solo performances.

I was the third in a series of psychologically stunted but malleable wives. I was far behind him—I didn't even know yet what kind of exorcism I required.

I found the classroom and stood in the hall for a moment, considering my entrance. The after-lunch smell of sweaty teenage bodies. The close feeling of an everyday classroom, the vibe of it. The long rectangular window beside the door had been covered in bright blue paper, showing only the shadows behind. I stepped into the classroom. The students, about eighteen of them, stood in a circle dressed in loose, earth-toned clothing. All the desks and chairs, except the large wooden teacher's desk, had been removed.

Their silence felt intentional, and I decided not to break it. I put my bag on the desk and stood behind it. I watched them. No one spoke.

## TRAINING

On a cue I did not discern, the students began moving in a circle, rotating as a group. Gradually, their movement evolved into skipping, and suddenly, in unison, they scurried randomly about the room. I didn't know what to do. Their seriousness and enthusiasm counted for something. Their open faces. The varieties of their physical manifestations: some compact and some gangly, Ethiopian or Irish or Central American, intensely present in their eyes or far, far inside. They began clapping in syncopated rhythm. They froze and challenged each other in strike positions. Music eked over the PA. The students were sweaty and smelled unwashed. I did not know how I could take attendance, so I left the attendance sheet on the desk and watched.

They lined up on opposite sides of the room and ran at each other, then stopped in menacing poses before retreating. One of them began dancing ballet. I was just the substitute. I could let them do anything.

I wondered if they were performing for me, or ignoring me, or rehearsing, or hallucinating.

I meant to tell them to sign the attendance sheet, but I could not betray their work.

The students ignored me. They raised their arms, then dropped to the ground, unmoving. I tried to discern who was leading the movements, since it couldn't have been choreographed. Suddenly they were all doing jumping jacks, then just as suddenly they stopped and pretended to be whispering to each other.

I took a piece of chalk and began writing on the blackboard. "Memory is greater than space," I wrote, opening to a page at random and quoting from the book I had brought.

The music had stopped; the room was silent except for the noise of the students' bodies moving in sync. I stayed at the desk. They leapt and touched their backs together in mid-air.

By now they were dripping with sweat—it clearly wasn't a game. It might have been some form of training.

"Hope is greater than memory," I wrote.

They lay on the ground and began rolling from one end of the room to the other.

Outside I could see a well-used path through the trees north of the building, and for a moment I remembered my own desperate adolescence: the woods, bottles, drunken mouths, friendships strangely full of insults.

The room stank of sweat and the silence was unnerving. We still had nearly thirty minutes to go.

They crawled on hands and knees back and forth, greeting each other from time to time. Their crawling slowed. One student in black tights and a green t-shirt seemed to be the leader. Then it appeared that another student in tan work pants and a white t-shirt was the leader.

I deduced that leadership changed according to some silent form of communication, and felt impressed by this. The classroom sat in the corner of campus, far from the other active classrooms; it seemed unlikely anyone would check in on us.

"Breath is greater than hope," I wrote, then went to stand uneasily behind the desk. It would be best not to mask my unease.

Music returned but I couldn't tell from where. It seemed they transformed into dogs for one moment, then swimmers. They inched along the dirty floor, now streaked with sweat, in a form of dry backcrawl. Then they hopped animalistically in rows, somewhere between a rabbit and an orangutang. Then a crabwalk.

*I dreamed about this*, I thought. Then I wrote, mixing my own thoughts with the book, "Do nothing original."

They crawled and grasped randomly, back and forth across the floor. They kept training, non-stop.

I liked the sound of their breath as they worked, how it seemed part of a telepathic exchange. I tried to count them and compare that number to my roster, but they moved too erratically.

Instead, I consulted the book again and wrote on the blackboard: "The self cannot be won by speaking, nor by intelligence or much learning." Could this be appropriate, in a school?

Their movements became more individualized, though built from a shared vocabulary. The student in tan work pants had curled into a ball and rolled around randomly. Two others appeared to be rowing a boat. A few made long steps forward into deep lunges. Were they carrying something imaginary? Others performed somersaults, or walked on their knees, or side-stepped. They never stopped moving. Sometimes they copied each other, or traded gestures.

Out the classroom windows I could see mostly a mass of cement-gray clouds hanging over the woods.

One student wearing a thinly striped black and white t-shirt stood and began rotating his arms, windmill fashion.

"The mind is the patron of the sacrifice," I wrote, though they were too focused to read a blackboard. Then again, what did I know about their capabilities?

I wrote "The infinite is bliss."

Minutes passed, breath by breath and gesture by gesture. Minutes were the reality of high school, not grades or knowledge or relationships or even words. The students sped up or slowed down and sweated.

Near the end of class, a student in a heavy-metal t-shirt began laughing forcefully, a fake, staged laugh. Eventually another, busy turning the crank handle of an invisible machine, joined in. More sporadic laughter spread through the room, on the edge of cruelty but also on the edge of genuine humor, or at least companionship.

I smiled too. Laughter is like that. I wondered how many of them were stoned.

They walked slowly toward the center of the room and gathered one by one, laughing. Some maniacal, some with generosity, touching each other on the shoulders, and they gradually got down on the floor. I watched and realized each of them was touching at least two others. They kept laughing until, at an indecipherable point, the forced laughter evolved to be mostly real laughter. Then they were really on the floor laughing, and I laughed too, hiding it a little with my hand.

I ran a line through the attendance sheet and put away my book. The students breathed out heavily and their laughter went out one by one like candles, until they lay in silence. It was over.

The clock read 2:30, though no bells rang. I picked up my bag and waved and said, "Thank you," sincerely, on my way out.

"Thank you," the students shouted back, which startled me a little. They were just kids, after all.

As I walked back across the campus, toward the graffitied fountain, I saw a student in fake leather pants wandering the grounds. He waved a tentative wave. He seemed to be working on a monologue for a production of some kind, speaking and gesturing to an imaginary audience.

Our paths slowly, awkwardly, intersected, and as I grew near his words became intelligible.

"Human beings walked on the moon. They murdered each other in gas chambers. They dreamt together in the ancient practice of lucid dreaming. The evolution of the hand. I've dreamt in a quarry. I've dreamt in a hotel room. It was the same. The dream is another place of its own."

I stopped walking and listened.

"What are you doing?"

The student looked down at the ground.

"I talk," he said. "That's my job here." Palms up, shrugging. "Not to say anything special. But to talk. Do you understand the difference between talking and communicating? That is my course of study. My job is the talker. I am not obligated to listen. I am not obligated to speak in any specific language. I am not obligated to repeat myself or not repeat myself or to make sense." He paused and smiled, as if to allow me to catch up. "My job is to talk. What is your job?"

"I'm the substitute," I said. A bird circled over the parking lot on the other side of the building, riding a high wind unattached to our climate below. For the first time I considered the nature of my job. "I pretend to do whatever an absent person would have done." He furrowed his brow and nodded, considering this as he drifted away. Pretend?

I walked toward the main building, where a cat sat on the steps to the back entrance, staring at me. It closed its eyes and turned away as I approached.

I wondered if the students were still in the room, if they were still lying on the floor. But I had learned not to look back.

At the office I signed out on the same clipboard I had used to sign in. The same fit, black-haired woman handed it to me.

"What is your job?" I asked her, smiling.

She smiled back. "I am the guide. I guide people." She surprised me then by pulling out a pack of cigarettes and offering me one. I had heard no bells or intercom announcements since I arrived. I hadn't smoked in years, but there is a time, you probably know it, when the invitation to smoke appears as a vehicle to something larger and you feel you must accept it. Which I did.

I took the cigarette and followed her to a small side door, then out to a fenced patio—the smoking area.

She lit her cigarette then exhaled by tilting her head up and jutting out her bottom lip. She kept one eye closed as she did this.

"What is your job?" she asked.

"I'm the substitute," I said.

"Sounds lonely."

"And free." I was still holding the cigarette. I rolled it back and forth between my thumb and first two fingers. It felt wonderful, a tiny belly.

"You don't smoke," she said.

"I don't smoke. Anymore."

"You're the substitute."

"Do you think they are still moving around in that room?"

"That's their business," she said.

Grayer and lower came the swirl of cement-colored clouds.

"It's their class?"

"It's theirs. You have a license, which satisfies a requirement."

"I don't smoke," I said, and handed her back the cigarette. She smiled and stared up at the clouds with me and finished, stubbing the butt into a small silver pail filled with sand. Far off traffic from the main road made the falling and rising sound of modern life.

She took me by the elbow. "Let me guide you," she said softly. We walked back to the front office and said goodbye at the door.

In the parking lot a few pigeons made their soft music. I stood at my car and stared at the hammocks. The top of a book stuck out of one, a tennis shoe from another. Along the edge of the athletic field, far off, The Talker was walking along a fence line, gesturing. In the next car over a woman in a gray wool coat sat staring out the windshield. She did not look at me.

On the ride home I felt more alone; having it pointed out had brought it to the surface, to the skin. As I pulled onto the main road, I resumed my smiling practice.

# MESSAGE

At home I performed the tasks: I picked up my mail, opened a window, fed the cat, changed the litter, got out a snack. I was home. I sat in the chair by the window and stared.

The message from my ex-husband, our first communication for over a year, was brief and to the point. "My father is dead. They found him in the yard. The visitation will be this Friday. Tomorrow. I thought you should know."

I stared out the window for a while longer. His father, James, had once threatened to throw a full bottle of beer at my head. One of his children had restrained him. No one, however, had admonished him. "That bitch," he had muttered. His eyes had looked crazed while they soothed him.

I replayed the message, to hear his voice, all the familiar tones of it. To remember how it once made up the other side of my reality, my daily life. His dear and dependable voice. I felt the intense beauty of my marriage aligned with its inevitable end, the absolute tragic rightness of its passing, and to feel these things at once, and hold them in harmony, was almost unbearable. I lay down on the floor and watched a cloud pass through the very top of the window, then it was gone, like everything. Down there, looking up, I thought of the laughing students.

After dinner I smoked the last of the pot and sat in the comfortable chair, listening to music. I could do this because I did not have children. I'd had one abortion and one miscarriage. Cars passed along the street occasionally, and once a cardinal flew to the window and seemed to look in. I played old songs, from before my marriage, from reckless, alive times. I loved children. What was wrong with me, after all? The music thickened. I heard syrup in it, almost love, running down through me. It was good pot.

Then a memory, from eleven or twelve years ago, crept to mind. It arrived as a feeling first, like a wave creeping along a shoreline. I remembered an afternoon nap, on a green couch, with my ex-husband. It was the early days of our marriage—these were some of my best days. He was behind me, right arm over my chest, holding my hand, both of our heads on a small worn throw pillow, afternoon sun playing through a red maple tree in late summer, windows open and the sound of leaves in the breeze, our warm bodies in complete acceptance of oncoming slackness. I felt his breathing slow along my neck as we slipped toward our thick, almost underwater sleep. We drifted in and out of each other, it seemed, to the rhythm of mottled waves of light and the sound of wind moving the trees. Just bodies moored by the moment of our flesh in contact. If a car passed by, if a lawnmower started up, if there was a voice from the sidewalk, it all melted before it reached us. We shared a common bliss, were aware we shared it, and trusted the other to feel the same. Oh, we drifted.

The music ended. The cat walked into the room, looked around, and walked back out. I was in danger, I realized, of being swallowed once again by the past.

I looked at my cold, efficient couch. There would never be a nap like that now; there couldn't be, knowing what I knew about him, about men, about myself. But it hadn't been an illusion. Only one stage of getting to here, a moment of ecstatic passage like the bridge in a sublime song.

ATTENDANCE

In the morning as I sat at my kitchen table, awake early and reading, the cat rubbing and rubbing against my legs, the phone rang. I felt certain that it was my ex-husband and rushed through all the possible versions of answering and not answering. Was it his need or my need? Or both, linked by an invisible cord?

It was Renata.

"Rise and shine, professor," she said. "Want to go back for more social arts today?"

"Sure," I said. "Why not?"

"Lots of reasons not to. But a little paycheck doesn't hurt. Same time and place."

"Yes, I'll be there."

"I'll let them know. You should feel good about this—the students asked for you."

I did feel good. I felt strangely included.

"Renata, I'm out of Mary Kay. Can I come by after work?" Those were our code words. We probably didn't need code words.

"Sure, just call first."

At the school, I looked again for the hammocks but there were none. The Guide at the front desk waved me in, talking on the phone the whole time. "Our next admission period," she said, "is in May, for the following year. We interview. Are you able to come in?" While she talked, she handed me the clipboard and visitor badge, writing a note and passing it over the counter: "Do you need help?"

Was I that obvious?

Near the fountain a few cats searched for the warmest patch of concrete and one hissed a little as I passed by. The cats shaded toward wild and I imagined they perceived me as currents overflowing from a body.

I took the same route, past the fountain, much of it painted over with new graffiti. I looked for the quote about moving in all worlds but couldn't find it. The athletic field was littered with large plywood boxes, painted black, and on each box someone had placed a piece of trash—although no, actually, a realistic sculpture of a piece of trash. More detritus. In East Hall I looked around—no students, though I heard laughter from outside. I looked again at the hallway ceiling, and now I could see that the white-on-white design was not architectural or abstract, as I had discerned the first time. It was somehow a portrait of a man in ¾ profile. He looked familiar. Though not quite famous. I was late and hurried on to the second floor.

This time the door was propped open and as I approached, I heard very soft clapping. A hypnotic rhythm. I paused at the door and straightened my clothes and my bag. I tried to slow my breath. When I entered the room the students were seated in a circle, facing out, eyes closed, clapping very softly. It seemed a test—how softly could they clap and stay in rhythm, stay connected. I stepped quietly to the desk, put down my bag and watched. The air in the room felt charged by their concentration, but not tense. I waited. I counted them. According to my attendance sheet, one student was missing.

As before, I simply observed. This time the students made sounds using their bodies or their voices or by strumming long cables held between them, making and remaking rhythmic patterns. For a while they hummed and the humming evolved. When it became rhythmic the students gradually slowed, seeing how much silence they could include and still maintain the song. At times two students held the heavy cables between them while a third plucked. They never stopped—the song evolved over the course of the class and they watched and listened to each other intently.

I wrote on the board only once: "The self is a dam, a separation between worlds so that they do not run together." It was from the page I had been reading at the table that morning.

Sometime after 2:15 the music grew quieter and quieter until the students suddenly broke their concentration and became informal. It startled me—I was all at once relevant and in charge. One of them, tall and indistinct, handed me a flier for an event happening that night. It was titled *The Night of the Trembling Boats*. The invitation was just a slip of paper with a map drawn on it, plus a time, a meeting place, and a title.

"We're performing tonight in the woods behind this building. We have ushers at the main door to bring you out. But come early if you want to be able to see. No chairs. There's a clearing we use. We really think you should come." Behind the student, several heads nodded and looked at me encouragingly.

I nodded back. "Yes," I said. "I'll be there."

I heard two cats fighting outside. I hadn't taken attendance.

## HIGH

At home, I called Renata. If I was going to a student performance in the woods, I would need a little help. I asked if I could come and pick up my Mary Kay.

Renata said, "You can stop by, but Grant might be here."

Grant was tricky. He was an artist and I thought his art often verged on making fun of art. You had to choose: believe in art and believe in the work, your sincerity somehow risking foolishness, or dismiss it and stand on the outside of the joke, feeling hollow. He created a lose-lose situation, I thought. But he would say that was all projection, evidence of my own internal struggle. He was simply making material objects that I was providing a context for. So I lost again.

Renata's house was small and green and her back yard ended at a railroad track. The garage looked like it just needed one good push. Her yard, famous for its fireflies, rambled uneven and wild. I walked up, feeling guarded, but Renata was already at the screen door, inviting me.

"Grant's here too. I usually don't double up but since you know each other..."

"It's fine," I said, and walked through the kitchen to the tiny living room with the floral couch and the corduroy pillows and the seed art. Renata went back to the kitchen freezer, where she would fish out a pre-measured quarter bag. Efficient as a dispatcher, efficient as a dealer. I imagined she had efficient orgasms.

I smiled at Grant, who smiled back. "Renata has good stuff," I managed. He opened his eyes wide and nodded. Was he mocking me or wholeheartedly agreeing?

"And she's dependable," Grant said, "which is invaluable." Renata came out with my bag and I handed her some cash. Nice and simple.

Grant said, "I used to buy from this guy Smalls, on Main Street." Renata groaned. "What, I liked him."

"You would," she said.

"But one time I was living at Central and Broadway, you know that four-plex behind the sandwich place?"

I nodded. But I didn't know.

"And I got these pre-rolled joints from him. Supposed to be trippy and amazing."

I wanted to leave. It was the start of a story, and I had the feeling I was being tested. I sat there like an idiot.

"I had this downstairs neighbor named Bob Ginkel. He was the king of the drunks. They all gathered at his back steps."

"You mean that guy who walked like a monster?" Renata said, and Grant nodded.

"I was feeling generous when I got home, and I gave him one of the joints. I go upstairs and I'm getting ready to settle in for the night, you know—sweatpants, movie, takeout, smoke up—when I hear sirens. Getting closer. I look out my window and they're parked below, taking Ginkel out on a stretcher. What the fuck. I found out later he smoked half the joint and his heart started racing like a cheetah in heat. The worst part is, three days later he's out of the hospital, he comes up and knocks and asks if I have any more." Grant laughed, but as he laughed, he watched to see if we were laughing.

Then a small silence descended on us. I stood up, Grant stood up, Renata stood up. We were all just standing there.

"I'm going to a performance in the woods," I said. "I'm going to go home and smoke a little first. I don't want to be late."

Renata was happy for our business, happy to see us leave.

Outside Grant said, "Wanna try mine? You won't have to go home."

"I don't live far," I said. But I realized it was another invitation of communion and nodded yes. The stoner code.

I tended to avoid Grant because he knew of my ex-husband's art, though didn't know him personally, and because when Grant was a junkie, Renata told me, his girlfriend Emily, *brilliant tough Emily* said Renata, shaking her head, became a junkie too.

I had met Emily once, at a party. She was sloppy drunk and singing "Thunder Road" while someone played guitar. I thought she was beautiful.

Grant ushered me over to his car and we got inside. He cracked the windows, produced a lighter, packed the pipe. Offered me the first hit, following the chivalrous custom. I should have moved further from my old life. I had thought crossing the state line was significant but what did these imaginary lines on maps ever do for us?

## AUNTIE

On the drive to the school I noticed the edges of things. Trees in outline, the little scalloped bullet holes in the road signs, the faux chrome trim of a car ahead of me. I was a distracted driver. Birds flew across the road in front of me and I could see their round eyes. I began driving unusually fast. I tried my smiling practice, but my brow stayed furrowed, and I imagined it looked disconcerting, even maniacal. My jaw ached and I kept having to relax it, massage it with my hand to keep from clenching up.

*What the fuck Grant. What the fuck did you give me.*

Whatever it was, it would have a name. Auntie or Bam-Bam or even just Chronic.

I tried breathing through my mouth. Clouds pressed down and moved quickly across the road in front of me, but I tried not to notice. How far was it to the school; how far was I from the moon—I knew that once! Every bump on the county highway sent a little picture of the road up through my spine and into my mind. My sweaty grip squeezed the beautiful steering wheel. Not to be noticed. Not to be noticed. I was so happy to reach the turnoff.

On the little gravel road through the trees and up to the campus, I saw lighted creatures floating in the woods. Part of the show, I was sure, and felt impressed.

A group of students and parental looking adults waited by the main doors, and an usher was going over the program and audience etiquette for the evening.

The usher was, of course, the Talker.

He saw me and smiled, or smirked.

"Follow me," he said to everyone, and we awkwardly fell in line behind him. He talked: "It is my pleasure to bring you to the show. Let me speak a few words. Talking comes from the mind and the breath. The students in this show tell me that *The Night of the Trembling Boats* is meant as a ritual of passage from one state of being to another. Actually they told me a lot of things. For example, that death happens inside eternity. That thoughts are always affected by friction from other thoughts and distorted by them. That mysteries are the most beautiful things. Anyway, please stay back from the clearing during the show. There will be no Q & A. Expect moments of radiance. But no flash photography, please."

He kept on talking, past the fountain and the ceramic trash displays, different at night, and toward the fence behind East Hall. At a point near the sidewalk, the fence had been cut and then decorated heavily with synthetic flowers, a portal or a parody of a portal. Fucking Grant.

Past the fence we followed The Talker/Usher on a path through the woods, lit by electric candles in paper bags. In the center of the clearing, delineated by a rope, a fire burned in a large kettle surrounded by stones. Shadows flared around us from the firelight. We stood for a while chatting and nodding and looking around and becoming accustomed. Then the crowd became quiet as crowds do in their extrasensory way, and some students moved through the woods, chanting and humming all around. That same chanting from class.

I looked at the circled audience, two or three deep at the edge of a large clearing that must have been maintained for these purposes. That's when I saw James, my ex-father-in-law, standing a quarter of the way around the circle, watching the dancers enter. The performers clapped with that rhythm they had practiced so earnestly this afternoon.

When I saw him, I first noticed how weary he appeared. As if he had climbed a thousand steps. The fire illuminated the side of his face and it was pale, bloodless, as one might expect. His eyes darted toward me twice, though he tried to stay focused on the performance. We stood, shifting occasionally, on the rough ground of the woods, facing in. I felt the dark sky above as a way, a conveyor. I had the momentary feeling that I could walk into *dark sky above*, that I could become more real there. Then I remembered that James was dead.

The students mostly used movement to convey the two shores and the trembling boats. Maybe one shore was life, and one shore was death. Maybe we shuttled between them, afraid of both. The performers spoke occasionally, and among the words they spoke, repeated and rearranged and deconstructed, were the words I had written on the chalkboard.

But I couldn't stop looking at him. The students climbed in and out of boats or graves or bodies, and pleaded with each other, then they broke down the words, into syllables they exchanged as gifts. It was a ritual, the Talker had said. And what did they mean by passage? And where was the night in which we were real? I stared at the side of his face. Finally, he turned to me, annoyed, and put his finger to his lips as if shushing me, though I hadn't spoken. He shuffled two steps back, out of the light. I didn't know how he had climbed the thousand steps; he seemed so weak.

The dancers moved in and out of the clearing and they sang to us, came up to our faces and sang sweetly right to each of us, rotating counterclockwise. They believed in something so much, but I had no idea what it was. The leaves seemed to sing also. Then the students filed out and they sang from behind us, circling again. It was like we were their little babies, hearing a lullaby. They stopped and we clapped and I became confused. Why would Grant do this to me?

Then I stood alone for a while at the edge of campus, darkness almost full, holding my keys in my right hand. I was so high I was trembling. I heard the keys shake.

On the ride home I found a radio station playing classic country music. My lifeline. "We're gonna hold on," by Tammy and George. I remembered my aunt drinking coffee at the kitchen table, that song coming out of a plastic fake wood-grain radio, the smell of pig manure on her shoes, the leaves and trees outside the screen door as much a part of my life as any person. "We're gonna hold on." I pulled out of the parking lot and tried to smile.

## NEWS

It would be a mistake to call him. It was always a mistake.

I checked the clock. Almost eleven. My fingers dialed, though not my mind. I didn't do it with my mind.

"Hello?"

"Hi. It's me. Sorry to call late."

"Ok."

"Thank you for notifying me."

Silence.

"I know this sounds wrong, but I wanted to tell you—I saw your father tonight in the woods."

Silence.

"I'm sorry. I don't know why I felt I needed to tell you."

"Are you asking for my help with something?"

"No. I'm so sorry for your loss." I hung up. He wasn't interested in his father's ghost—that was like him.

Words kept disappearing into the past then reappearing through portals. That was it. I thought of moments and people and animals and houses I had loved. How lucky I had been to have these things to love. How I might see them, even briefly, again, and feel what I had felt. Or a new feeling. This was wonderful.

The cat jumped at something and then pretended it hadn't. I picked up the book on the kitchen table. I read "From the dark I take refuge in the dappled." Nothing made sense. I paced and made tea and sat awake until the light changed gracefully into morning, thinking and rethinking my scrambled thoughts.

## FINAL

The last time I subbed at The Northwest Academy of Arts and Social Sciences I was in a state of extreme doubt. This happened from time to time. The doubt started small: *Had I seen a ghost? Had I been dosed?* Then it generalized: *Is the border between realities extremely porous? Am I sane?*

Monday morning following the students' performance, Renata called.

"Once more, with feeling. Northwest Academy," she said.

"Renata, I've got to talk to you."

"Sure, let's make an appointment."

"Tonight," I said. "I need to talk tonight."

"Give me a call. I'm around."

As I drove I forgot to smile. Low, heavy clouds raced across the sky. I remembered being the students' age and how it felt. I wasn't like them at all. I conformed to the standard rebellion of the time. Remembering those days felt like looking through a telescope, seeing just a small circle of reality, close-up and isolated. I saw myself riding in a pickup truck with my boyfriend, a six-pack of beer on the seat between us and we talked about nothing, excited about nothing, just the hot night, windows down, drinking and driving along gravel roads. A good song on the radio thrilled us and that was as deep as we got.

I smiled at The Guide at the front desk. She was just so bright and present. I said, "Guide me."

She smiled back, produced the visitor badge and the clipboard, asked, "Did you like the performance?"

"It freaked me out," I said.

She laughed and said, "Must have been a good one. I never go. I only work during the day. That's it."

On my way to the classroom I stopped to look at the ceiling. The designs I had seen before were merely cracks in the old plaster. That was plain and clear now. As soon as I looked at it, I remembered James, his finger at his lips, shushing me. That fucker.

My ex-husband, too, always asking me to wait.

When I entered the room, the students were already writing, mostly while sprawled on the floor. Their faces shone inward with concentration. I watched the search inside their minds play across their faces.

They wrote in silence for 45 minutes. I watched. I read the book. I remembered how lonely I was at their age, how moments with friends or boyfriends that were supposed to alleviate the loneliness hadn't even touched it. And I wondered about my ex-husband, how that too had crumbled. Because how could I really love. Where would I have learned it?

Tears were running down my cheeks so I turned toward the corner of the room.

*Shit*, I thought, *I'm The Weeper*. What a terrible job to find at this outpost of fringe behavior. The students continued writing. I sat behind the desk, my back to them. I wept. Someone had carved a small cartoon angel into the chalkboard frame. Out the windows, clouds and crows and leaves blowing around.

When I had wiped my face clean, I turned around and they were staring at me.

A goth-looking girl sitting near the desk asked, "Are you ok?"

I said to them, "I think I'm The Weeper," and I started laughing.

They smiled but then they waited. No one said anything for a bit. A tall transgender student with bright orange hair said simply, earnestly, "Why are you The Weeper?"

I threw up my hands. "Maybe because I've started to live more in the past than in the present. Or is it more in the object than the subject. I don't know. It happens. Maybe it's ok. But you should know about it. It could happen to any of you."

They didn't buy my elder wisdom routine, and I didn't either.

The girl in the front, her dark, glittery makeup streaked from her eyes to her temples, said, "Nobody cries more than me, and I'm not The Weeper." The students nodded and laughed in recognition.

A window rattled from down the hall. We listened to it together.

"Ok, I have to tell you something." Space in the room condensed, it seemed. All of us there in the room to get through life.

"I saw a ghost at your performance. A person who'd been dead for three days. And he saw me too."

They nodded slowly, taking it in.

A tall boy in the back said, "Yeah, I've heard about that. I've heard that happens sometimes at these kinds of things. Rituals."

The goth girl said, "Is that why you're crying? You miss this person?"

"Oh hell no. I don't miss him. Maybe it's sad that he was so cruel, but that's on him. I'm probably crying because I'm this old and I still don't know my job, to use your terms."

The girl smirked. Everyone else seemed in on the joke.

"What?" I asked.

She shook her head. "Umm, you just told us you saw a ghost. You're The Seer. Duh. You see things, right?"

I felt in my body then a bright pool. Of course, yes. The Seer. Still I resisted.

"Why would I cry then?"

The students guffawed and shook their heads. They seemed, as a group, in disbelief of my ignorance. The tall boy in the back said, "The Seer is always an outcast. A woman Seer especially. They're like, tragic. It's a tragic position. No one is willing to change their reality for *your* information."

These children. Class had already ended but they didn't care. I thanked them and told them I would think about it.

"Think all you want," said the goth girl. "Seems like it's not really up to you."

Outside the classroom, I saw the maintenance woman pushing a cart toward the end of the hall. She peered back at me and I waved.

The Guide was waiting for me to sign out. It's just that she was smart and funny and I liked her. How simple. I thanked her and felt like kissing her hand. But I didn't.

From the parking lot I saw the Talker walking far along the fence line. Practicing, I suppose.

I resumed my own practice of smiling. What the hell. At home I performed the comforting tasks. The cat needed my lap, the mail was nothing, really, I opened a window.

At 4:30 I called. "Renata, Grant dosed me and I saw a ghost."

"Ok. Slow down. Dosed with what? Where did you see it?"

"Out by that school. In the woods." And I told the whole story to Renata, who listened and made little reassuring noises of assent, each a gift. I imagined her looking out the screen door and taking a hit from her pipe and checking the cupboards for some dinner. I sat in the comfortable chair and told her all of it.

"Ok. There are two things you should know. First, I don't see how Grant could have dosed you, because I don't sell that stuff and after you smoked with him, he came back in. Said he forgot his lighter but I'm pretty sure he was just horny. And no. Anyway, he didn't seem extra anything. Second, you're talking about Singing Woods. Weird shit happens there. It's a well-known fact."

The dog two houses down barked wildly, and the cat stiffened, and someone from across the street yelled *Shut up.*

I could hear Renata moving around in her kitchen, distracted. I told her, "Ok, ok. One more thing, though. This isn't the first time I've seen something."

"Really?"

"Really. I think it's just the first time I've accepted it."

"Well, that seems like progress, doesn't it? Shit, it's raining now. My stuff's on the line."

"I'm a Seer," I told Renata.

"Yep," she said. "Good luck with that."

I picked up the book. I read "The one who sees things here as various goes from death to death." Maybe it wasn't the right book to be reading. Music drifted over from a neighbor. Or someone was playing the cello. Or sighing. Or the wind.

# THE STORY OF
# HENRY FORD

WE LIVE IN a house hidden deep in Singing Woods and we receive few visitors. People tell stories about us, and some claim our family to be an abomination. But we consider our reclusive lifestyle a form of devotion. *Our house is a temple*, we often say. Magical occurrences abound, though rarely for the better.

Normally, it is just the three of us: father, mother, and me. Though tonight father is out rambling, and we have a visitor named Henry Ford. Honestly, I am quite tired of him.

And now as evening grows late I discern that Mother and Henry have been smoking hashish in the cave. I smell it on them when they return and it is the smell of springtime. I imagine there to be a hookah. Henry Ford comes back glassy-eyed and Mother returns wearing a big smile. I have a strange mother. At times she can be quite trying.

"Henry," I say, "it's getting late. The woods aren't safe at night."

"Pass the spaghetti," he says. He grins and pauses to listen. Together we hear flitting sounds in the nighttime woods. "Like you mean it!" he says and stares off again.

I have set the table as is my duty. I have put the situation in order. The fork, the honey pot, the napkin in its metal ring. I have portioned each space for civilized behavior.

I do not like eating to be haphazard.

Mother walks into the room. "Dull," she says.

So Henry starts singing. He has expressed a desire to return to the cave and smoke more hashish. But instead he sings opera on the living room floor in his dusty black coat. He gets down on one knee then reclines all the way to his back, one hand outstretched to the ceiling. He wails away.

Father will be home soon. I am nervous. Father is a brown bear. *For home father goes.*

Mother discovers she has lost one of her earrings, perhaps in the cave. She stands up, holding her dress carefully, and makes her way along the path behind the house. I hear her sing in German.

Henry goes quiet, as do I. We are alone again in the ticking house, beasts all around us, including father. Winter had entered the woods suddenly, as a coyote rushing through. But Spring enters by incremental shades, as a lizard inching up the wall.

Henry, still on his back, says, "I have decided to eat you," then he laughs. "Very slowly!" He laughs even harder, he can't stop. "I'll eat the whole house! The whole decade!"

I wish father were home. I begin clearing the table. "No! No!" says Henry from the floor, but he can't get up. He has hashish legs. Out the kitchen window I see a bear, lumbering up the driveway, stopping occasionally to tell a little secret to a fern or honeysuckle. I hear mother's lilting German. I see the stars over Singing Woods, where we all live and eat and dream. And Henry's voice, too, circles above the glow of the house.

Morning leaks into the lamplight. The loose beast on the lawn. Blind sleep overtaking Henry Ford. Henry crying and automatic and losing his language. Henry on the floor like a tipped-over confessional booth. Henry heartache in the dirt turning infant before his lord. Henry knotted hot and going dormant, and the bear who sleepwalks up the driveway toward him.

I am just the son of these disasters. I am just a little firework far in the night to Father bear and Mother dear.

Wake up Henry, against the tide of Spring come to douse your dream, a Model Zero falling into Henry Ford on the flowery floor dreaming his own hand in its old story working weird light across the ceiling. And the door opens. And father is home.

I am afraid father will eat Henry Ford. I watch him assess the situation. He sniffs the air, certainly smelling the Hashish. He hears mother's singing from the cave where he sometimes hibernates. He looks to Henry on the floor and to me, clearing the table. Father says, "What is that sweet light from Henry Ford's ribs?"

I offer my father a plate and he waves it away. Henry Ford mumbles something in false Italian. His grin slackens as he aims his mind toward dream. The house is clean, I am happy for that. All three of us seem to be waiting for mother. What a terrible burden we must be on her.

Already I understand this about my life—there is no place for me except off to the side. I picture a sort of spirit play in an alcove of the temple, made mostly of minute gestures. I am the silent understudy.

Father ambles forward and slumps on the sofa, laying out his long body. He looks depressed. Henry has gone to sleep. Father says, "I want something, I picture it, I hold it in my mind, then when I see it for real, when I can finally touch it, I don't want it anymore. What is this condition?"

We have assumed our positions. Henry on the floor, horizontal. Father on the couch, diagonal and lumpy. Myself, upright, vertical and mobile. A theatrical arrangement, I think. Meanwhile a shift in our darkness arrives. Slight movement in the leaves and grainy particles of light. It's going to be one of those dissolute, unending mornings.

Father speaks quietly, to himself, "The yawning gulf between self-perception and our actual place in the food chain will undo us. The poetic future of the corpse appears in the living body." He looks Henry over. "The circular nature of non-being. The folly of our intentions, as if talking to a sundial and expecting our voices to act as light." He is simply working his mind.

I take note of each sound. I count them to myself. 1. Our house as it settles. 2. Father's voice. 3. Henry's restless shifting. 4. A nightbird. 5. My own breath. 6. Wind.

Finally mother returns, her eyes bright, lifting her dress as she hurries up the path and into our cozy home. In the lamplight her flush face gleams. "I found the earring," she announces, holding it aloft. "I find things."

Father's bulk trembles. He appears pleased with Mother, and nods, but from an alien mind place. Mother stops behind the couch and observes our tableau. I watch her face sink in recognition. Her sudden eyes. She comes onstage then, into our drama. She has snapped into character.

"Well, what should we do with him?" says mother. Her shine shows its wear now.

Father says, "If I eat this Henry Ford, another will surely appear," and he yawns.

Henry twitches in sleep. As any simple transient being. I start to count the twitches because I enjoy counting. The fire needs a piece of wood. Henry has twitched four times. Father fights back another yawn.

Mother looks down and says, "I've lost the earring again." But she is holding it in her hand.

Father says, "I suppose Henry Ford is like my shadow or something. I suppose I should look at this with the intention of learning from it. I just can't see why I have to keep dealing with him. It enrages me, if you want to know."

The stitching of our family, if you look closely, is very rough. It could unravel. Now there is an after-dinner smell to the room. Grease in still water and unsatisfied, gurgling bodies.

Henry seems to awaken. His eyes water and he stretches out his mouth. Henry the dusty black-coated baby. He is our guest.

Henry looks at father, spread across the couch. He looks at the burrs in father's fur and the long tongue hanging out of father's mouth. He looks at mother and lifts his head.

"Your husband is a swine?"

None of us know what to do with Henry, his oncomingness, his disorientation, his mechanical rhythm. Henry is crazy. We imagine he will own Singing Woods, and us.

Father laughs. "Does a swine have fur like this, Henry?"

Mother tidies the room nervously. She joins the salt and pepper shakers in the middle of the table. She neatly arranges the fire poker and ash shovel. She clears her throat, rough from the hashish in father's cave.

"My husband is a brown bear, Henry. I'll ask you to respect it."

I make myself very small in the room. I have developed a trick of shrinking my energy and of standing very still.

Light just now inching up the walls. Nighttime melts slightly, the darkness turns gravy-colored and the trunks of trees outside grow more distinct.

Henry says, "Helen, why would you marry a bear. You know they are going extinct."

Father's eyes flash at the word, then he relaxes. He clears his throat.

"What is our purpose here, Henry. What is the purpose of a single blade of grass or a bumblebee or one human being?" He shifts his haunches on the old couch. "Or one bear."

Mother looks at me and motions with a tilt of her head that I should leave the room, but I don't move.

Henry says, "Our purpose is to fulfill the will of God."

Mother and father laugh, by reflex. Henry, still on his back on the floor but slowly sobering, arches his eyebrows.

Mother moves to help Henry to his feet. Father straightens himself. I feel a presence in the room, rushing forward. Henry will make us lose our ability to speak; he will turn our woods into gardens. He will steal father's handsome youth. He will find the bean inside us and reproduce it. A telescoping feeling that our room has advanced in time but we have not and Mother helps Henry to his feet and dusts his jacket, and Father rises on the couch, slobbering, and I stay very still in my corner while the room spirals into the century and changes shape and color and Singing Woods fades to a panel of scenery.

Just a moment of this, a fleeting passage of this feeling, then Henry begins his goodbye speech.

He pounds his legs and chest as if to regain feeling, then speaks. "We must overcome this darkness. This weather of fate we find so… sculptural. Like trees. All around us. Helen, and family. I will speak to you about the development of savage and fantastic cities in which the repetition of the spirit is no longer chained to the cosmic cycle. I am going there. It is the beginning of the end of the animal within and the animal without." He looks at father and blinks. "We are about to leave both the cycle and the fragment. We are about to live permanently in eternity. Not heaven, but eternity."

Father begins to growl a little. Perhaps he is hungry, or uncomfortable. I have the urge to bring a pillow for his shoulder but I don't move. Henry ignores the growling. He seems aglow.

"I have to leave you. It is an act of spiritual freedom, leaving Singing Woods. I am not like a wheel. I am what uses the wheel."

Father slowly rises to his haunches, his nose searching the air for a smell. I have seen this behavior before. Mother's eyes widen. She says, "Dear, be polite. Our guest is relaying his philosophy."

Henry says, "We do not work for the dead. They are too slow. We are water and they are dust. It slows us down to carry them. And Helen, animals are lazy. I admire them. But our task finds expression in the city. Our future…"

Father moves unbelievably quickly now. He springs from the couch and in one more leap is at Henry's chest, knocking him down. Henry's scream emerges garbled as if echoing from a well. Father tears bits of flesh from Henry and growls deep in his throat, as if unable not to growl. The sound of cloth ripping. Father whips the shocked body from side to side and holds Henry down with one paw then pulls away with his teeth at the meat of Henry Ford. While Father rages I try to escape the room. I find I cannot.

I try to remember the cave, how mother had once bundled me in coats and blankets and carried me from the warm house out to the winter night. Stars above and the bare frozen trees. Up the path toward the cave where Father slept. I try to remember the sound of her boots on the snow and how the sound seemed to move through her body and into mine.

Then kneeling, holding me close to her chest where the smell of mother and sweat and woodsmoke swept in through the blankets as we crawled toward Father. He slept in his cave during cold months and we visited him, curled up against his fur, each point of it needling my neck and palm. *Father, do you dream here? Am I in your dream?*

We curled next to his warm fat body in the full joy of mammals pack-sleeping in cold. Oh father. *Squeeze the pads of his feet*, Mother said. *He can feel it and he knows we are here. Say your name*, Mother whispered to me, and I did. All this in a flash.

Oh Father.

It is done. Henry twitches in pieces all about the living room. Father sits back and begins cleaning himself. He licks his paws and bites at the burrs on his haunches. He shakes his great head and the muscle and fur ripple down his back. Mother moves automatically, in shock but competent, practiced. Now we must follow the script. Father has written it, without a word, or we have written it for him, shaped around his silence and suffering.

Mother comes out of the kitchen holding a rattle she has fashioned from a husk and some seeds. She shakes the rattle in a quick rhythm. Father flattens his ears onto his head. Mother sings quietly, one of her no-words songs. Just humming and sounds from the rhythm of the rattle. A lullaby.

What a burden we must be. And she is a wonderful singer.

Henry's bloody, twitching torso settles a little, becomes less person and more meat. Mother sings.

Father stops cleaning himself and returns to the couch. "I'm sorry," he mumbles quietly, more to himself, more inward.

Mother shakes the rattle. It is almost morning now.

I will be helping to clean up the parts of Henry Ford. It is not an appropriate task for a boy my age, but our house sits deep in shadows of the hills and is our temple. Occasionally sacrifices are made in a temple.

Father curls on the couch. He looks as if he will sleep soon, the heavy-lidded eyes and his mouth, inclined to yawn but still bloody around the snout. I walk to the fire and add a piece of wood. Mother's song drifts through the room, quieting us and all of the woods, all of the world it seems. Who is Henry Ford anyway.

He is the recipient of a lullaby, guiding him in death not to haunt us. His goodbye speech had actually been a huge success.

I sit down by the fire, close my eyes and try not to see father's muscular neck ripping the body of Henry Ford into shredded tendons and meat. I listen to Mother, like a good boy, but cannot escape. *Father is not right in his devouring* I think.

The sounds from Henry's body as it deforms in the growing quiet.

In these fragile hours after a kill Mother and I sleep shallow; Father sleeps as if under a heavy weight. I wonder how he dreams after the shocks of adrenaline have exhausted his system. I like to think he dreams cleansing dreams but when I ask father he only says, "I don't remember" in a wistful voice. Father and I are different. Father is a bear.

I hear everything now. Every unsettling sound.

Father sometimes tells his hibernation dreams. He tells them in spring. One year he said, "I dreamt the cave led down to a pool filled with wine, and animals floated in the wine, calling for help. I tried and tried to help them, but I could not reach them. There was no way to help. Then I realized I was being called to save them by drinking the wine and I laughed. It was spring! And I was so thirsty."

Eventually Mother sleeps in her bed and Father sleeps on the couch, which he always does after an outburst. I get up and find pieces of cloth and flesh in all manner of nooks and crannies, and the general torso of the body is nearly too heavy to carry outside for the crows and bees and ants to have their way with.

Two hours ago I had been talking to Henry Ford and now I carry his decapitated torso across the threshold of our home and out to Singing Woods. The dragging sound, the leaking body scraping over roots and through leaves. We live in Singing Woods because it welcomes anything cursed. We do not have to decide if father is our curse or we are father's curse. Here we can just go on.

Night birds echo loudly in Spring, before summer heat dampens down our passions. We are marginal, interspecies, anachronistic. Father teaches me these words so that I will learn to stay close.

The woods aren't safe at night.

I have accepted this feral side of father abstractly, but each time I witness him in bloodlust the images persist longer and longer. I fear I'm developing avoidance mechanisms.

I pull the torso one lunging step backward and rest. I do this twenty-seven times until I am far enough from the house. I leave the body in some shoots of wild ginger and last year's leaves of scrub oak, for our friends to clean up.

Mother sleeps and Father sleeps and even Henry Ford participates in a kind of sleep, headless and eternal, but I sit awake as daylight filters through the canopy of Singing Woods where it seems as though nothing will ever change.

In the body, some cells of Henry Ford are probably still living. Oxygen rushes in to the exposed parts. Somehow, the ants and flies, even at this hour, become aware of the body. I move away from it. I move away and finally I sleep curled on the porch and awaken to bright noon of almost Spring, held at bay by the unfurling canopy of Singing Woods but also tainted, outlined by a worn-down feeling in my body.

Our woods tell the marvelous wet story of Spring. Commonly known as desire. I walk into the house and mother is cleaning, whistling. Father sits with his coffee, humming a different, older song. I look out the window and see another Henry Ford, walking up the path. His black coat clean and pressed. Birds flutter in the trees as he approaches, a wave of disturbance and animal light preceding him. Henry smiles and calls out to us. Father sighs. He is so tired of it all.

# BROTHER AND SISTER

## JUNE 10

We were taken to the athletic field in small groups and asked to look at the sky. Some of us saw monstrous shapes in the clouds; we were asked to discuss the shapes. We stood shivering in pajamas and boots on the new grass of the uneven field. Beneath the bright cold of the spring night, the depth of summer eased toward us. I said, "The clouds look like the tops of giant trees. That drift around." An attendant wrote this down. Our rehabilitation had begun.

One of my new roommates cornered me on the way back to our ward. We stood near an empty bulletin board and looked down the long, beige, cinderblock hallway. "Did *you* see sparks coming off your boots out there?" he asked. I hadn't. He gestured with two fingers, as if holding a cigarette, and shook his head in frustration. "We gotta stick together. Do you know why you are here?" he asked. I thought he might be testing me, but I wasn't afraid of him. I said, "I don't know. It will help me not become a criminal, I guess." He shrugged and looked around nervously.

I went into our room and lay on my cot. Rustling noises and the smell of bodies at rest. Just before I fell asleep, he came over and knelt near my head. He said, "My name is Westy. You didn't ask me my name. You gotta work on that." He patted my arm and walked away. But he hadn't asked my name either.

## JUNE 11

A kind, elderly man in blue coveralls walked me down the hall to the music room. I hesitated, but the attendant there, a woman in white coveralls, motioned for me to enter. She nodded toward the piano and said my name, as a question. I nodded back. She asked me to wear a gorilla mask and play the piano. For an awkward moment time crawled past. I didn't know how to play the piano and told her so. She told me, "Just do your best." I sat down and put on the mask. It smelled new, molded rubber and factory air. The attendant sat behind me with a clipboard. I was not to look at her. The shine of windowlight revealed scuff marks on the linoleum flooring. The piano sat perpendicular to the wall, a tall upright, out of tune. I began to play. I did my best. When I stopped playing the room grew so quiet I could hear the nurse writing on the clipboard. She said, "Very good. Don't turn around. Play again. Play who you are in the mask."

## JUNE 14

I asked Westy about intake and he said, "You don't remember the snow fence or the bus ride or the clipboards? Oh man." He shook his head sadly at me. We sat on our cots, filling out our personality tests. I began making cartoon shapes by darkening the bubbles on my answer sheet. One question asked if I had ever seen a spirit. But did they mean separate from a body, or trapped inside?

That night I lay in my cot and thought of ways I might contact my sister, who must have been in re-education too. We grew up in the same fractured household; we were 'at risk.' I tried to remember the social worker taking me for a car ride. And the large holding pen, and then the bus, all of us stunned and bouncing along. Had she been there? I couldn't remember our first breakfast. But I remembered how Westy and I started talking and smiling and trying to appear hopeful. How we kept our talk coded and referred to any time before this place as My Old Life. We would say, "In My Old Life I used to..." and make a dumb joke. As I fell asleep, I imagined the voice of my sister calling me names. *Shithead. Dork. Idiota.* It calmed me.

## JUNE 15

In the afternoon I was taken to the 'computer room' for a test. I sat in a tan office chair facing a computer and a series of numbers flashed on the screen. A man in white coveralls asked me to repeat the numbers and I did. Each series of numbers was longer than the last, and I repeated them until I made a mistake. Then I started over. I feared I was being trained for a new vocation. The attendant said, "We are just testing your memory." His tenderness surprised me.

## JUNE 17

I was called into a small office and told that from now on my treatment would be unique, based on the results of my personality test. The test had revealed that I was angry, but the attendant who told me this—a short, stocky woman with round glasses and a very short haircut—said they didn't know yet why I was angry. She explained that as part of rehabilitation I might be asked to stack salt pellets, one by one, into a wheelbarrow. Or place a stack of empty rain boots into a pleasing pattern on the front lawn. In group, we might choose an everyday object and make a papier-mâché replica of it, one hundred times larger. She watched for my reaction as she said these things. I might be asked to imagine, before entry, that our sleeping room was a garden. I might then be asked if it was becoming a garden. I might be asked to balance an oar with my eyes closed and walk in the field.

## JUNE 19

Today in group therapy, the first discovery of my treatment: I have a narrator. The events I experience are described in my head as they happen, by a voice that is not exactly mine. It's self-generated, so technically it is my voice. But it's not the voice I use when speaking aloud and not quite the voice I use when 'thinking.' I told the group that I had at least two inner voices, and that one of them, a narrator, could comment on the other and could see me in third person, but from inside. I had always thought this to be the case for everyone. The other group members stared at the floor or their hands. The attendants raised their eyebrows and looked at each other meaningfully.

On the way back from group Westy cornered me, leaned forward, elbows out, eyebrows knit together, too serious.

"I hear you've been asking people about your sister. What's the deal?" he said.

"Do you know her?"

"I was talking about you." He jabbed his finger into my chest. "What's the deal with you?"

I felt helpless and just watched myself from another angle of the cafeteria.

He said, "I don't have a sister." Everyone at the nearby table was pretending not to listen. Westy relaxed a little, aware of his threatening posture and the people watching. "It must be cool."

"Sometimes." I said.


## JUNE 20

This morning I had a vision of running away, through strange woods, surrounded by distorted, upright animals. Suddenly I jerked awake. Westy saw me and came over. He knelt next to me and calmly patted my arm. He told me he never dreamt. Because this was the dream, and there was another life he was already living. Maybe better, maybe worse. He patted my arm again and winked.


## JUNE 26

I had been walking for about an hour, wondering if self-narration was an illness or a special talent or just normal. Rocks near the creek glittered as clouds broke open. I saw one of the calm, kind attendants, Bradley, standing near an old wooden building. Perhaps guarding the door or perhaps on break. As I approached, he smiled from that unreachable position of rehabilitator—disarming, bemused, caring, somewhat inscrutable.

"Do you like it?" he asked. His blue coveralls had grown thin and shiny at the knees.

'What? Do I like what?'

He laughed then gestured to the building behind him. He was thin and graceful. When he swept his arm toward the building, I was sure he had once been a dancer. Or that he was dancing right then.

"The barn," he said.

"I love it," I said, without knowing why. I hadn't really considered the building at all. "Can I go inside?"

"Of course," he said. "I'll take you. You have to be careful, it's very dark."

He pushed the door open and we entered a small chamber created by a black velvet curtain on a semi-circular track, smartly fashioned to block the light. I grasped his elbow as he held the curtain aside and led me forward. The darkness of the barn surprised me. No light came from between the wallboards, and I heard faint humming. The barn was cooler than it should have been—somewhere a cooling system held the temperature steady despite the day's growing heat.

"Follow my voice. The floor is level." I followed him in a circle around the barn. My eyes adjusted slightly but there was little to see—vague walls, a shiny floor, perhaps vents in the walls.

"Alright. Keep coming. Walk at a steady pace."

I did as instructed. "What's this building for?" I asked.

The humming had a calming effect. I could sense Bradley's shape ahead.

"What do you think?" he said.

"I don't know." I could see almost nothing, though for a moment I thought I saw a streak of purple light move diagonally, toward the ceiling.

The floors were made of wood or vinyl, not concrete as I had expected.

"Is it for dancing?"

Bradley was silent for a moment. "It could be," he said.

The barn intensified presences. The quiet developed a presence, the dark too. Even Bradley's silence became many-sided.

When we returned to the vestibule Bradley helped me out the door, into the slight heat. We stood in the glare, blinking at the multiplying faces of budding trees. Alive again.

I could feel the altitude. It must have been break time for some of the others; more than a dozen men and women in blue coveralls loitered near a pile of rubble, some of them smoking. Behind us the barn seemed transitory as a cloud. I could hear it humming, alone these miles into the wild sky.

"What's my job going to be here?" I asked. He shrugged and took a cigarette from his breast pocket with that same melancholy grace.

He said, "You have to decide." He looked me over from behind the cigarette.

My uncertainty extended to all categories; I wasn't even sure what they meant by a job. I smiled at him and nodded.

Bradley asked, "Did you like the barn?" I nodded. "Did you see anything?"

"No." I said. "What do you mean?"

He shrugged. I turned to walk toward the main buildings, and Bradley smiled and nodded, gesturing with his head to indicate I was going in the right direction.

## JUNE 27

In the morning I found clean underwear and coveralls at my cot so I put them on. My roommates groaned awake inside our collective, hovering smell. Westy was singing *I'm Popeye the sailor man.* In the corridors dim light washed over grainy, peeling cinder block walls and asbestos tile flooring. I sat in the cafeteria and watched the others. *Was this really my life?* Out the window I saw a hawk, high and still above us, meet the wind and look over the open athletic field. It balanced there. Far below, some field mouse had no idea.

I did not know the goal of my rehabilitation. Had I missed something? I assumed that through re-education I would become more useful. Also, that some of the patients were spies, or more kindly, secret observers. Westy agreed with me, grimly.

As I watched all the strange people eating and chatting, I thought I saw through a cafeteria window my sister, walking away across the exercise field. I was certain it was her—pale white girl with her delicate walk and strange haircut. I stood to return my tray, hurrying to catch her. After navigating the return line and the length of the cafeteria and the double doors, I walked out and could not see her. The clouds seemed tied to shadows and raced across the field. I stood in front of the building and turned in a slow circle to calm my mind; I made a thorough, organized visual search. Here and there people crossed the field. Wind from the south brought warm, humid air. I began to doubt that she could be here at all, that she even needed rehabilitation.

## JUNE 28

I walked to the fence and looked out across the dilapidated athletic field. Beyond that, the ground sloped gradually toward distant villages and the tree line began in earnest at the uppermost edge of Singing Woods. I'd heard stories about that place and knew not to wander.

Two women in blue coveralls passed by and I gestured to them. They walked toward me with such ease, arm in arm. I couldn't look at them and hid my eyes. All my furtive life I did this. They stopped and waited.

"Do you know how I could find someone? My sister is here," I said finally. I felt that the pleading tone of my voice marked me as desperate; I made a mental note to conceal that tone. The women looked at each other with puzzled faces. A great sidelight shone on them from beneath the clouds.

"I guess you could try admin," said the shorter of the two. "It's right there, anyway." She nodded, squinting toward a low brick building just across the field. The windows there seemed sheets of fire. I thanked them and walked toward a gray metal door at the near end. *What is life anyway*, I thought.

Inside the building a large man with sideburns, wearing coveralls and holding a stack of files, approached me. I stood rabbit still, until our pause became unbearable, then managed, "My sister is here somewhere," which caused him to puzzle further at me. He turned and pointed at a small sign overhanging a door, reading "reception," and I thanked him. He stood watching as I walked to the reception office.

The receptionist, who was kind, could not help me. He sent me to another office labeled Center for Excellence. There, I was sent to another office, where an older woman told me to sit down. She smiled a kindly, inhibited smile, the trademark of this place.

"Are you the finder?" she asked, possibly as a joke.

"The finder? No. I'm terrible at finding things."

"Why is that?"

"I lack independence. And 'initiative.' I've heard." I waited for a minute. She silently exuded grandmotherly calm. "I'm looking for my sister."

"Are you ok?"

"My sister's here. I saw her. Can you tell me where she is?"

"I'm sorry, we can't release the names of any participants. It's a privacy issue."

"But she's my sister. We're family."

"I'm sorry. Why don't you talk to Facilities Services." She directed me to another office, this time in an adjacent building, smaller and with glass block windows.

When I arrived, they were expecting me.

A man in a tweed coat gestured to a chair. He began speaking about privacy, and the confidentiality agreement all rehabilitative and psychological treatments require. He said that he himself had no idea if my sister was present this summer, or if I even had a sister. He only knew that I should focus on my own rehabilitation.

"How did I get here?" it occurred to me to ask.

"You were referred for treatment by a consortium of family members, education professionals, and municipal officials. Just like everyone else."

It sounded like a scam, but in other ways it made sense. I had been suspended from school and then arrested for slashing tires. I had been sleeping on friends' couches and floors and my family didn't seem to mind. Most of the time I just wanted to hide, preferably in basements. Once in a while I slept in the backseat of an unlocked car, for the thrill of it.

"I'm on your team," the man said, and led me to the door. "Don't worry about your sister right now. Just find your job and be helpful."

But I always worried about my sister. Mostly I worried that she couldn't see me. That she didn't even think she had a brother. I walked out into the sun feeling a little stunned. The hairs on my arms cast tiny shadows. The man from Facilities Services thought we were on a team together—the world and its powers were actually kind of stupid. I had thought it was only me.

## JUNE 30

I returned to my cot after group to find that Westy had been sent home. His cot had been removed. No one knew why, but I listened while two other participants speculated that either he didn't need rehabilitation, or he had been found incapable of rehabilitation. What else could it be?

"He could have committed a crime here," I said. "Or been a spy." They stared at me for a while then left.

I sat on my cot and closed my eyes. Darkness rushed toward me. My legs wouldn't move; I leaned down onto the blanket and right away I dreamt. Something about being dead but still having to go to school. When I woke, the dream evaporated. I remembered how people in the dream had shivered when I talked to them, then I was shivering in my cot, awake. I listened to animals mewling outside.

# JULY 2

Again I found myself at the barn. I walked the perimeter once to be sure no one else was there. I waited in case I had been followed. Birds circled far overhead, almost invisible. I wondered how they could survive so far into the atmosphere, and what they could see, and if they were real. There were less trees here, just thin pines and strange, reedy birches, decrepit, unlike those in town. I loitered, hoping to look casual, then tried the door and it opened. I stepped into the little chamber, pulled the heavy curtain aside, and called, "Hello?" into the dark.

Gradually my eyes adjusted and I saw, in the center of the room, two women seated on either side of a stream of light, dressed in peach coveralls. They interpreted the light with their hands, or they directed it. Or was it light—it illuminated so little and appeared textured. The substance, or light, streamed between them and disappeared upward. They didn't seem to care that I was watching; they remained engrossed. Their hands did not quite move in unison, and the tension of their disunion sent small ripples through the substance. At first, I couldn't see the chairs the women sat on; their bodies seemed to float. They performed this service, I intuited, for the people at the camp. I was overcome with gratitude and stepped outside. Daylight blinded me and I shut my eyes for a long dizzy moment. When I reopened them, there was Bradley.

He smiled. I shaded my face with my hand and said, "I think I found my job."

"In there?" Bradley asked.

"I would like to help the sisters who translate light."

Bradley laughed. "That's what you saw?" I nodded. He shook his head. Somehow Bradley's coveralls seemed tailored to fit, almost stylish. He said, "You won't likely see the same thing again."

Confusion crept into my face and Bradley smiled. Behind me I imagined the two sisters directing the stream of energy, day after day.

"You kind of have a sister thing, don't you?" said Bradley.

"No," I said. "I don't."

## JULY 4

I stood at the fence, looking out at Singing Woods. Everybody had little secret histories, I thought. Their own catalogues of supernatural phenomena. What was the mind anyway. Mostly a source of shame.

One night long ago, in my parents' basement, I'd heard voices from the television when it was turned off. I crept behind it and unplugged the cord, but still heard the voices. I stood with the plug in my hand, leaning my ear toward the window, wanting the voices to be from the yard or street, but they came from the television.

The next night I cut the valve stems on the tires along a line of new sedans in the Ford dealer's lot. I was caught, of course, and ordered to pick up trash by the roadside as part of a redemptive spectacle.

Before that, I had once spent a sleepless night listening to a face in the ceiling as it chanted. I lay there, immobilized, imagining my promises and supplications toward the face; a light that had grown in my mouth obstructed me from speaking aloud. For a while I convinced myself this was a dream.

And even earlier, one day in the park where the river oxbows (I think I was very young) I saw voices rising from pine trees in wavelike pulsations distorting the air. I could not hear the voices, only see them and feel their pressure against my cheek and forehead. I felt like a luminous antenna.

I gripped the fence railing and threw my head back. Nothing moved in the woods. A voice could come from anywhere.

## JULY 6

Bradley told me the barn conducted "imaginal being." Or images from states of being triggered by our consciousness. We were walking along the creek toward the main campus. "It's not in your mind," he said. "It exists already whether you do or not, but the presence in the barn is co-creating images with your consciousness so you will understand it in pictures."

"But I don't understand it," I said. He smiled his sly stage smile. A field mouse darted from one rock to another. Trees hummed.

## JULY 12

I had discovered a small limestone bluff, mostly hidden from view, overlooking the buildings. I could see where Singing Woods started, and here and there a chimney or a clearing. Deer and wild turkey moved along the wooded edges, on dimpled, beaten paths. From the bluff I could watch everything without feeling self-conscious.

My rehabilitation program had been personalized. This felt both humiliating and satisfying. I attended group therapy but was able to design my independent growth program (IGP), and for that I frequently chose solitude. I had been going to the barn, sometimes twice a day. It was unlike me to be so focused. If the barn was occupied or locked, I waited in a hidden spot to see who came to unlock it, or who came out. I developed a routine. Group therapy, the barn, exercise, lunch, the bluff, Bradley. I began to feel that I inhabited an empty pocket of time, a cul-de-sac in some eternal struggle, and this felt like progress. I wanted Bradley's attention constantly.

## JULY 14

A small bright light grew at eye level, some six feet from me. I heard a cry and jumped. Bradley took hold of my arm and I grabbed his hand. My own hand came alive with sensation then, in the dark. Each nerve in my arm grew a new awareness from the heat of Bradley's hand. His touch was like a drug.

Bradley squeezed my arm and whispered, "What do you see?"

"I see a baby. It's floating there. Don't you see it?"

"How many eyes does it have?"

"Two. Of course two. Why?"

"Wondering."

We stayed still. I could not tell if he saw anything at all. I could hear his breathing and feel the heat from his body. I said, "I guess I can't see the top of its head. There could be more."

"Good thinking."

He casually released my arm. My body vibrated, awake to everything.

A baby crying. Was that all I was?

# JULY 25

Bradley had become my primary individual counselor, overseeing my IGP. He waited outside. The hill country was heavy with impending rain, but the barn stayed cool and dry as always. Some leaves had blown to the doorway and I tracked them in. Bradley was watching. I was a fuck-up.

Nothing happened, so I closed my eyes and waited. When I opened them, I could see a metal painted bed frame and mattress, old, like a farm bed, floating above the floor. A plain white bedspread covered it. Emerging from the bed, as if from underwater, a swimmer, a young woman in a white rubber swim cap. Her shoulders came around in a butterfly stroke and she dove back under. She swam in and out of the bed like a needle in a sewing machine. She made no progress. I watched her swim cap emerge from the bedspread, her shoulders, all of her body moving past until her ankles submerged, then feet, then her toes disappeared and it started over. I watched and watched. I tried not to admit that it looked like my sister. That it *was* my sister.

Afterward I asked Bradley to follow me to the ledge and we sat there looking across the compound to the woods. It felt daring and vulnerable to show him my private refuge. I told him about the swimmer in the bed.

"Do you swim?" he asked.

"No. No way."

We sat in the quiet afternoon light and watched crows all around flying in the same direction, toward a stand of taller trees near the river. The beginnings of a congress.

"Why not?"

"Obviously because it's fucking dangerous."

Bradley shook his head. "A lot of things are dangerous. Riding in an airplane. Having sex. Driving a car."

I stopped thinking. There on the ledge, in my private, hidden refuge, Bradley had mentioned sex. In the abstract, true, but I knew that the body finds a way to communicate. I was too excited to speak.

## AUGUST 3

We sat in a circle of folding chairs in one of the classrooms, monitored by a gray-haired woman in her mid-fifties, wearing large glasses and blue coveralls. Like so many of the attendants, she held a clipboard and glanced at it from time to time.

"The topic is shame," she said. "I hope the readings were helpful. Each of you will speak." Then she waited.

I shifted in my chair and looked carefully down at each hem of my coveralls, noting that one, my right, was more worn along the bottom than my left, and wondered if it meant that one of my legs was longer than the other or if I actually walked with a limp and did not know it, if in fact I had been born with a physical defect that no one ever mentioned or if, somehow, I had known this but forgotten, and what else I might have forgotten about myself, and if my rehabilitation was about remembering, if this place and this program was what happened to people who forgot who they were and must undergo either the process of remembering or the process of inventing a new self, appropriate to the aims of our society.

Still no one spoke. While we waited, some kind of mountain bird called out. Another low cloud bumped past. I wondered about the barometric pressure, what that even was.

No one spoke. She waited.

A man wearing a nametag sticker with "Lawrence" written on it in capital letters began tapping his feet, then realized it and stopped. He looked down into his hands.

A far-off greeting to someone named Risa, shouted from the athletic field, reached our window, faintly.

Finally one young man gestured almost imperceptibly with his right index finger to indicate he would speak. He cleared his throat.

"I am ashamed," he said. More silence.

The attendant nodded encouragingly as if to say, *go on.*

He looked at a shiny spot on the linoleum floor, in the middle of our circle, and spoke intensely to it. "I'm ashamed of the way I've treated the people I love. This is not the person I want to be."

I tried to place his accent. It wasn't like I could discern a Russian accent from a Ukrainian accent, for example, or Honduran from Guatemalan. Or even Texas from South Carolina. I was an idiot, actually.

He started carefully. "I have not been truthful. I have told them I was going to one place, when I had no intention of going to that place."

We settled in.

"Sometimes I said mean things to a girlfriend, so she would feel bad about herself and not be strong enough to leave me." He kept on— cheating, abortions, women slapping him in parking lots, police knocking on the door at 3 a.m. A dim green aura grew around him as he spoke and hardened there when he stopped.

I had resolved never to speak in therapy, but now a strange rising action, like yeast or peonies or carbonation, moved the air inside my throat. The group leaned slightly toward me like tall grass in a breeze.

"I stole money." I looked down. "I slashed tires. I stole liquor too. I beat up Mike Everson in the locker room at school." My right leg was going up and down like a piston, all on its own. "I don't know why I can't control myself. Also, I have a narrator. And I have visions." They stared at me.

Everyone waited for more.

"It's hard to describe what it's like. I think there's something wrong with me."

I thought about confessing that I was attracted to Bradley. He seemed like he would be an excellent kisser. But where's the shame in that? The group looked into their hands. I sensed they were embarrassed for me.

The attendant looked closely at me and said, "What do you mean, a narrator?"

## AUGUST 10

The afternoon temperatures grew stifling and I began walking the creek upstream each day after lunch. Beneath my reflection I saw crayfish, backing into the mud beneath stones as I loomed over them. I wondered if summer was getting late; time here was constantly being disrupted. Improbable realities were everywhere.

Westy had left a cryptic note under my pillow. It read *The deepest attachments are to forms of silence.* Had I really been there more than a month?

I tried to understand it, sitting on the small, crumbling, ancient ledge. People below crossed from building to building, or weeded flowerbeds, or stood in circles learning to breathe in unison.

I wondered if my purpose, my job, could be to encourage others to seek visions. But that couldn't be right—I would have to talk to people, be convincing, and I had no such ease. You don't just find your job laying around somewhere, I thought.

I watched the routine of the compound unfold below me and thought of the hallways and classrooms at school, the peculiar smell of bodies and paper and pencil shavings, florescent light bouncing off floor wax, thin metal locker doors ringing shut. I thought about going 'home' and the ambiguity of that word. Where the woods stopped, birds took over, dazzling everything. Below them the compound stood like a purposeless, blind church on the road to oblivion. The trees stood at the edge of a wasteland or the edge of heaven, depending on your view.

## AUGUST 13

"What is the visionary task?" Bradley asked me.

"To shepherd," I replied, dumbly, having no idea. I had no gift for prophecy—I might as well have been watching sitcoms when I received the visions. Bradley asked if having visions gave me the urge to tell people about them, or to help others receive their own.

"No," I told him. "I just have visions."

"But how," he asked, "will you use them to contribute to your fellow humans' growth and well-being?"

"I'm just trying to get better," I said. "I'm basically an antenna."

I went away feeling stuck—a vision wasn't an obligation. Though even the crows had a congress and exchanged information. At best, I felt destined to act as helper to ineffable tasks. Someone in a side alley who reads auras for ten dollars.

## AUGUST 18

On my way to group therapy I saw Bradley walking toward me with a petite woman, not in coveralls, who shone as if a special clearing in the sky followed her. I waved him over, and he introduced me to his girlfriend Marina. She spoke in an accent from someplace and I would never know where. A sunny place, I assumed.

Marina said, "Did you hear the singing outside the cafeteria?"

I hadn't.

"It was the song of the serpent and the torches," she said. "Really cool."

"Oh that," I said casually.

The light they stood in seemed filtered through another light from the past. All around us little bites were being taken out of reality. Dragonflies wove in and out of the air above the athletic field. Seven sparrows flew together to the top of a fence then down to a patch of grass. I counted them. The creek and the trees and the birds made a sound together that obliterated language.

Bradley said, "I was looking for you earlier. We think your rehabilitation is nearly resolved. Insofar as you are ready to work on your narrator and practice your vocation in the institutions and landscapes of public life."

"Resolved?" It was like a strange term from a biology or chemistry class.

He shrugged. "We think you are about ready to take your work here back to your life at home." He gestured with his hands as if my 'work' were a loaf of bread being moved from one shelf to another. Marina stood awkwardly by, looking over at low clouds tumbling along. She was probably a better visionary than me.

I said, "Maybe my job is to let dimensions pass through me and report their feeling to everyone."

Bradley said, "Well, that's kind of grandiose," and smiled. "But you know that."

One day in the barn I had seen a man in a strange hat who seemed helpless to communicate. He appeared sideways and smiled in a resigned way, almost embarrassed that I could see him. The fur trim of his hat sparkled. He seemed like a passenger, pulled through time by unseen forces. I remembered smiling back at him and felt I was in that same position now, giving that same helpless smile to Bradley and Martina from my strange world.

For a moment, I thought I saw in Bradley's eyes some acknowledgement that he had played me. Or did I just think everything was about me. Or was his erotic attention merely part of the rehabilitation after all.

Their auras were just normal air, at that moment. Bradley and Marina. Some part of me, high in the fantastic reaches of the brain, was devastated. I changed my mind about the quality of his kisses.


AUGUST 23

I asked the van to drop me off at the high school, even though school was not yet in session. From there I walked aimlessly. Strip mall storefronts shone. I went into the dollar store to do some math and calm down. Twenty percent off from 3.98 meant what. Four giant candy bars for five dollars meant that each bar cost $1.25. The lights in the store surged in rapid waves. The cashier was reading a book. Her aura spiked inward.

At some point I began walking home. It seemed strange, ghostly, to just appear there. At the park near my house I sat on the swing for a while, listening. Leaves, squirrels, passing cars. I was a person who had completed rehabilitation. I felt like a stranger buried inside a stranger. Yet still better, even, to be that. The way home passed too quickly. I walked up the steps to the porch. No one was there. Each chip of paint, each weed in a crack of sidewalk, shone in detail. It was like a map or an old game board. Someone had put me down on this square and I was waiting for them to roll the dice.

## SEPTEMBER, IN GENERAL

That fall, when I returned to school, everyone said how much I had matured. "It was the waterboarding," I joked, and no one laughed. I doubted I was the first in our school to be rehabilitated, but the process still made people uneasy.

In English class we applied rhetorical strategies to our arguments, in physics we measured angles of refraction, and in algebra II we showed our work while solving for x. At lunch we complained about the scoops of mashed potatoes and we pretended our tiny milk cartons were opera stars. Everything seemed normal, but there existed an outline, a trepidation at the edge of people's eyes, little reassuring glances containing hidden questions no one could interpret. Or it had always been that way.

From the perspective of our beloved and numbing school, visions were a manifestation of sickness. Our survival required sustained denial of the multiple and swarming nature of realities; it was exhausting. I wandered through the days. At times voices still whispered, though I managed to ignore them. People noticed my attentive ways, my calm wariness. I was in training.

The girl with the locker next to mine said, "Most white boys need re-education anyway. That seems obvious." I nodded. I couldn't argue. Her aura was filled with crackling electricity. I walked the halls between classes, hoping to feel the intelligence of the universe. I rarely spoke unless asked to speak. I watched and stood to the side, urging people toward their fullest expression with my eyes. I felt advanced to have this secret purpose.

My sister noticed the change and didn't trust it. She still saw me as the kid who stole her underwear and hung it on the antenna of the kitchen radio.

### SEPTEMBER 9

One day, sitting on the front steps at home, I watched my sister walking up the street toward me. She hadn't seen me yet. She was looking down at the boulevard grass and as she walked, her lips moved. She talked to herself, I realized. She didn't have many friends. She was small and alone, an oddball like me, just hanging on, inhabiting this reality only partially.

Around her I saw a shell, protecting her. She was tough. Her toughness was her beauty. The shell around her never stopped moving and it intersected with colors, beings, textures of light.

She stopped suddenly when she saw me.

"Creep! Why were you watching me!" she said.

"You have a beautiful shell around you," I said, expecting more abuse from her.

"That's right," she said. "I got that and more."

I said, "It looks like that stuff they put in guitar necks."

"Mother of Pearl."

"Yeah, it looks like that, but sometimes also like fur. It's so cool."

A pigeon flew from the top of the streetlight. Together we watched it walk around at her feet, cooing. Its feathers shimmered when it entered the shell of her strange attention. It wasn't afraid of either of us. For the first time in a long time, she looked me in the eye and smiled.

### SEPTEMBER 18

I begged my sister to take me back to the compound, though I wasn't sure where it was. I remembered my sightline from the limestone bluff, and retained a general feeling of direction and elevation, but the exact location was a mystery.

When my sister graduated, that was it. She would be gone.

She had a driver's license, and her friend Darren (whom she described as a "massive stoner") owned an old brown Delta 88. She had already borrowed it a couple of times.

I told her there was a place in the compound that conducted interdimensional magic.

"Interdimensional magic? What are you, eight years old?"

"You'll see," I said, trying to sound confident and mysterious. She rolled her eyes.

Since re-education, my visions had been unpredictable and often arrived at the worst moments. In gym class, for example. Or once when my social studies teacher asked me a question, I saw around his shape an image of multiplying feathers, rotating like the track of a bulldozer. The poor man. But how could I concentrate? I began to feel cursed by my new vocation.

## SEPTEMBER 23

My sister was busy planning her escape but eventually I wore her down. It was the biggest favor she had ever done for anyone—borrowing a car and giving up her valuable time for, undoubtedly, a fool's errand. I offered to pay for gas, which meant I would steal the money from mom's purse, not her.

I packed a lunch of ham and mayonnaise sandwiches and potato chips for both of us and managed to shoplift a bag of knock-off 'sandwich cookies.' Then I lay awake in bed, imagining another life.

## SEPTEMBER 24

We got up early, both looking bleary, wrinkled, unaccustomed. Thin daylight lay in a film across the yards and trees; long shadows haunted the neighborhood porches and alleys. The broad, brown seats of the Delta 88 smelled intensely, insanely of smoke. It was like floating along inside a giant ashtray.

We were happy at the start. Me with my map and my stash of cookies, and my sister maneuvering the long, archaic car through quiet streets.

It was the most time I had spent alone with her in years. We talked about whatever we saw, almost breezily, almost without a care.

Once we got onto Route 18, I kept guiding us up into hills until we passed a creek and turned off. A wall of trees developed along the road, then fences, then the road turned to gravel. I remembered that sound, and the cold air beneath the canopy. It seemed familiar. The magnetic pull of the visions themselves, as beings in their living dimensions, probably guided us.

Even though the bluffs and the creek and mailboxes and ditches all looked the same, I found indicators here and there. At one point I watched a giant jellyfish float into the woods but didn't say anything. I thought how it rhymed with the low clouds. Just as we began to tire, turning short with each other, my sister noticed an old sign for a defunct community college, and we followed it on a hunch.

Then a feeling came into me like my skin was remembering itself, and we turned down a road and I knew. When we pulled into the compound my sister said, "Oh, you were at this place," as if she recognized it from legend. I exhaled a tense breath. Only two other cars sat in the parking lot. My sister parked as far from them as she could, and I took out the sandwiches. Cold air reached into the car. We put on knit hats. We ate our sandwiches together in the front seat, slipping potato chips between the bread and munching in silence. The administrative building flickered under passing clouds.

"Come on," I said. "We just follow the creek." I shouldered my bag and headed up the empty path.

"What's in the bag?" she asked.

"Stuff. More food. Supplies."

"Why are you bringing the bag?"

I shrugged. A familiar pine tree waved. I grew more nervous as we walked, and my sister grew quiet. She had retracted something.

I noted little changes in the creek, a newly downed tree, and felt the pleasure of knowing a place, how memory does arrive first in the skin, then seeps toward the brain. Weak Autumn sun laid its washed-out light across images from my summer. But when we arrived there was no barn. Only a flat, uncovered rectangle of dirt. Could it have been a temporary structure? I stood where the doorway had been and felt little stirrings in my stomach but only that. My sister turned, head bent upward, and watched some birds floating along above our exposed, tiny bodies.

"The building was right here. It's gone," I told her.

"What do you want to do?"

"We should go to the ledge."

I led her along the trail and down to my precarious little landing. We sat and acclimated, looking at each other and nodding. She took a pack of cigarettes out of her jacket and held out her hand. "I left my lighter in the car."

I dug in my bag, setting items on the ledge and making an exaggerated, grim face. My sister picked up the can of lighter fluid and looked at me.

"What the fuck. What the actual fuck."

I sighed. She just always knew. "I was thinking of trying to undo the curse," I said. As soon as I said it, I heard how stupid it was. I knew I couldn't have done it. I probably couldn't even have gotten a fire started.

My sister made a sound like a snorting, hooved animal and balled her fists. "Did you not think this would implicate me? That I might lose my spot at the U? My scholarship?" She fumed and shook her head and clenched her fists again. "You fucking idiot."

"Things seem different sometimes. I see how stupid it is now. I don't know."

She looked at me like she didn't recognize me at all. No, like a person who knows you very well, miming that they don't recognize you anymore.

"What happened to you up here?"

Then, instead of crying, I told her everything. I told her about voices in the television, nights awake talking to the ceiling, the barn. All my little crimes. I even told her about the crush on Bradley.

She was quiet. The two birds were still up there, and a small, distant part of her was still watching them. I became aware of a next level of cold, creeping through the rock ledge toward our bones. Together we stared over the treetops. When she looked at me her face trembled. My tough sister. I waited and she smoked, hunched over, legs dangling.

She shook her head slowly. "The way I see it, there are four possibilities." Her eyes narrowed. She was working this over inside. "First that you are completely looney. You should be locked up. That's possible. You know about Dad, right?"

I nodded, but I didn't know.

"Second that you were under the influence of a person or drug and your experience of this place is not reliable. That is possible."

She paused a while to consider her words, staring far off but also inside herself. My toes tingled with cold. "Third, the barn was a temporary structure, erected and removed each year for re-education, perhaps in storage here somewhere to preserve its magical properties. A *delicate* interdimensional barn. Christ."

I could see a flash in her face while she talked, a giveaway that she was stating this possibility only to be kind. Perhaps patronizing me. I thought I might be the only person who could still find her buried kindness.

"And fourth, the barn was never there—it was a vision too." She thought about this. She blew smoke from her cigarette up, up, into the sky above.

We sat together on the ledge and I felt impressed by her and I was happy. Mostly because of how much she was talking to me.

"I think it doesn't matter now," I said. "I think I'm just here."

"Meaning?"

"I learned something in the barn, but I didn't learn how to deal with it. Now I have to learn to deal with it, just in everyday life. I don't need the barn to be real to do that. And you are almost the only person I trust in this world."

A person might someday become a fossil on a ledge, a vision seen from another dimension, dust, a weed, an asteroid, almost anything. Far below, I saw movement in the trees. A deer stepped from woods to clearing and stood shining its long face all around. Wind rose toward us. I closed my eyes and listened. I heard it all. It was terrifying.

# THE STORY OF
# EATING THE KING

IN THIS KINGDOM, the following are considered errors:

Failure to use a king when the world should begin with a king.
Omission of a period of time belonging to a king.
Omission of the king's name during birth contractions.
Omission of a king who always belongs between you and the world.
Failure to acquire a sense of futility when thinking of the king.

*the king and momentary illusions*

The king sat under a tree looking at a little round beetle. He hardly
heard the queen come by. The king fell asleep on the grass, cupping
the beetle in his palm. He lay still and looked very cute.

*the king avoids a topic*

Everyone in this kingdom has a little book of his or her own in
which a record is kept. Each month we must bring an appropriate

gift to the king. Instead of respect, we give him money. About this the king says nothing.


*the king and the ever-living now*

The king jumped up on a table and tried to escape. The queen called it a disgrace. We may have a new king soon. We wonder if he will act with similar selfishness.


*how to eat a king*

When one slices into a king, precision is unimportant. If the king is alive, an anesthetic such as cannabis or opium may be administered or withheld, according to the pleasure of the eaters. The eventual goal is the spirit.


*fragmentary legends of the king*

In the beginning an eye blinked.
In the beginning there was too much flailing.
In the beginning the world was a horsefly looking all over the universe for something to bite.


Then the king began eating his sons. The king started to turn into an asteroid, just a little bit. The king's hair caught fire and would not go out. Whenever the king spoke, normal hair began to fall out of his mouth.

*the origin of the king*

    *part I: where we found the twelve princes*

We found one floating in the swamp. We found another in a field when we were waking up the animals. He was kept warm by their bodies.

I said, "Look at this, the king has left his babies everywhere."

We found one in a sack, out in Singing Woods.

Someone else said, "How many queens are there anyway?" We had other questions, too.

One of the bakers found a prince in the flour bin.

All the princes were hungry; all of them were babies. And though everyone loves a baby, there's only so much to go around.

We built a pen for the king's sons and fed them what we could. At times their angry cries or pleading looks were too much to bear. We felt ashamed. Honestly, at times we treated them like livestock.

They brought us together in service but also in guilt and resentment. They were difficult babies, telepathic and nasty. As one began to crawl, the others watched. Soon enough, princes crawling everywhere.

Sometimes people passing through town asked about the pen full of children. All those baby boys, growing wild together, can that be healthy? Some people suggested we drown them. How much trouble will a pen full of feral princes bring?

We knew they were right.

We found one in a stable. We found another in a flowerbox. The discovery of princes kept on like that for some time. Our lives took on the quality of a scavenger hunt. One day I saw a prince in the squash patch; at first I mistook his head for a small gourd.

We found the tenth prince at the top of an oak tree, in a crow's nest. A woodcutter saw his little leg dangling over.

We found the twelfth in an open grave. Before we heaved the dead body down, the priest said, "Look, another baby boy."

Red-haired and blue-eyed babies, like the king. Birthmarks and other royal aberrations.

Many of us felt that a child who came to us from a grave was a sign. That he would eventually bring to us a curse.

The twelfth prince was the last. We didn't believe it for a while; we kept watch for another to appear. We found ourselves looking under a sleeping goat or sifting through a haystack before jabbing it with a pitchfork. We double-checked the wagons. We began to feel relieved, though still wary.

There were just too many princes. We had difficulty keeping track of who was who. Of the royal order of succession. Eventually we moved the pen into Singing Woods. We hid them away. We fed them goat's milk and cantaloupe. We tended them.

Then they started disappearing.


*part II: subtraction and the throne*

In order to ease our burden, we made a schedule for the feeding and coddling of the twelve princes, and we put the older children in charge.

The King was our supreme spiritual authority. But when the princes began disappearing we did not report it since we had not reported their appearances. We found ourselves in a bind.

One omission begat another.

They grew into toddlers. The pen became a cage. We watched carefully, according to our schedule, but each week the cage contained fewer princes. We stationed more children and an adult whenever we could spare someone, though we could not neglect our work.

Finally, one of the older children made her report. She had seen a prince disappear. It was quite simple. The other princes had killed him in the night, eaten the unfortunate prince and buried his bones.

From twelve princes, the number dwindled. We allowed it. In a month, there were five.

Some of us, shamefully, began to watch. Some of us played favorites.

The toddlers' instincts for violence astonished us. Royalty is exceptional, we thought. Perhaps even divine, the hand of an angry god.

Eventually we covered the cage at night and instead of monitoring them we guarded against their escape. Soon enough there were only three princes left in the cage. We listened to the cage in the night from our beds and heard their rustling and growling and wailing.

The lives of the princes oppressed us. Through a circuit of lies and missteps, we tended their violence like a crop. We couldn't look each other in the eyes. We began to use coded talk and euphemisms. We spent less time together and took meals alone in our houses.

Of course that final morning we found only one surviving prince. The watchers called out and I rang the bell and we gathered around his cage. He stared at us, blank-eyed. He presented himself as an innocent. I told the crowd, "It's important not to be afraid of him. He's only a child." By afternoon, we wondered if the other princes had ever been real. If perhaps we had been in the grips of mass delusion, well known to occur in our territory. And convenient.

Then, as befitting the normal progression of things, we presented the surviving prince, the twelfth prince, to our king. We knew he would become our only king one day. We returned to our lives. Eventually our king died mysteriously and the prince ascended. We tell this story to our grandchildren and they live inside a great fear, its own sort of cage.

*the king's actual story*

On Monday the king believed he was turning into an asteroid.

"I'll be cold," he said. "And I'll fly above you all, inspiring awe. It's much like now."

The members of his court listened politely then went back to their work: sewing, singing, eating, and fighting. He had once again failed to capture their imaginations.

Then the king's hair caught fire and would not go out.

"Why is this happening?" he asked the court.

"You are becoming a flaming death comet," said his son. "You bring evil tidings and seven years of doom unless we take action."

"I must be extinguished!" cried the king.

Enter the queen.

"The only way is to cut off your head," she exclaimed.

"But my head may continue flaming," said the king. "That's no solution at all."

The members of the court conferred. They would invite all in the kingdom to solve the problem of the king's head.

A lady-in-waiting blew on his head, which only increased the flame.

Then a jester urinated on the king's head, which did nothing to the flame but did amuse the court.

The knight put a helmet on the king to snuff the flame but the helmet began to glow and turn orange and burned the king's scalp.

The blacksmith was called, and the herbalist and the midwife. No one could extinguish the flame. Finally, out of desperation, the river man was called.

"What can we do?" the king asked. "I will give you one fourth of my kingdom if you can extinguish the flames shooting from my head."

"One half," said the river man, and the king agreed. So the river man in his black cloak, who claimed he knew something about eternal flames, took the king by the arm and led him out of the castle.

They walked toward the river. The night grew strange to the king. The river did not look its usual self. It seemed to stretch boundlessly on.

A boat rocked halfway up the shore, bow on land and stern moving gently in the water. The river man instructed the king to climb into the boat.

"Are you comfortable?" he asked.

"Yes, I guess so," the king said, surprising himself. The river man pushed off with barely a sound.

The king looked back and saw his queen and all the members of his court waving from the shore. They began talking to each other excitedly. It seemed they were having a party to celebrate his crossing. The king began to feel lonely, overcome, adrift. A great regret crept into his body, as if coloring it gray.

The river man said, "We have to put the flame back where it came from," and this made sense to the king.

"Where did it come from?" the king asked.

The river man smiled and pointed ahead, into the darkness, lit now by the king's flaming head. "The other side of the river," he said.

"I've heard of that," said the king. The river man smiled. Everyone said that.

The King waved back to his court from the far shore, but they appeared not to notice him. They threw back their heads and their laughter carried across the water. Once again he had failed to capture their imaginations.

*little king story*

In the distance of memory there lives a very small king. He repeats the same stories over and over, on a small stage, but the stories change slightly, imperceptibly, each time they are told. The little king begins again. He does not know if he has an audience; he can't see into the blackness beyond the lights.

*the story of eating the king*

We had thought eating the king would be more pleasant. This eating is in fact a labor of great pain and goes on through the night. We have employed the use of the bone saw. We have scooped the eyes. We have stripped the tendons from around the knees and ankles and we have pulled whole veins from the arms and legs. We have broken the feet. We have spread the ribs. We have cut the penis and we have pulled out the intestines. His spirit, however, remains elusive. It seems to escape before the knife. We have flayed the tiny muscles of the hands. We have hooked the spinal cord from within the vertebrae. A flock of birds gathers for scraps. We continue.

*the king's coda*

The king turns to wave back at us from across the river. We are in a different place. We sit with the body, realizing its slow passage through our own bodies. The king calls out but we hear only the gurgle of the river, the soft touch of leaf against leaf in the evening breeze.

# THE STORY OF THE MIRACLES

WHEN IVES WAS YOUNG, his parents had taken him, along with his sisters, to evening dances at the Wasioja town hall. His uncles Alvin and Edward were famous dancers; his cousins and sisters danced as well. A stout little band played old-time music from the stage: waltzes, polkas, schottisches. Each family brought a dish or two to share, and during intermission they all stomped down the narrow stairs to the basement to eat and drink and exclaim.

Up above, benches lined the sides of the dance floor and exhausted children often slept there beneath piles of coats. He liked it best in winter, when the windows steamed and then frosted, and he would come in from the stark cold to the close dance hall air and remove his coat and feel instantly the swirling human warmth of the dancers. His uncle Alvin lived across the street, and while he danced his wife Inez baked cinnamon rolls in their large kitchen, for the children. His grandfather lived up the road in a small brick hut heated by an oil stove. His oldest cousin Anna lived above the grocery store in a large and bewildering apartment. Only a few hundred people lived in the entire township. Winters threatened to wipe them away, but still they danced and worked and watched the baffling stars overhead. At one of these dances, Ives had seen a ghost.

He had walked outside, intending to cross to Inez's kitchen. But something had distracted him. In the bright moonlight he saw a man without a coat, his gray shirtsleeves rolled up, his red suspenders tight, leaning against a small brick building. The man was flickering. Young Ives walked to him in wonder, and the man slowly turned his head and stared. "Boy?" he said. "Boy!" Then he bent down to look, hands on his knees, and said simply, "It's a miracle." The man was strange to Ives, not of human substance yet ordinary somehow. Ives turned and ran, until he stood breathless in the kitchen where Inez was making frosting. "Right on time," she said. "Here." She offered a spoon and he licked it, trying to banish the old man in suspenders from his mind.

That was over sixty years ago. He remembered it often, and the memory seemed to grow brighter. Since retiring from his job as the school band instructor, he had lived on the old Albertson farm, a little more than a mile from Plainview. Wasioja itself, miles away and mostly abandoned, had also brightened in memory. The ruins of the old seminary. The civil war recruiting station. The south fork of the river shining in summer sun.

His memory stretched like a long, shapeless field, and he had time now to explore it. On Saturday, he thought of walking to town, taking the shortcut through the woods to listen to birdsong. He didn't want to become lost in the bright land of memory; he needed communion. So Ives set out through the woods at the South end of the pasture.

As he walked he hummed favorite songs from the old days in Wasioja. He found the muddy footprints of a fox and followed them until they seemed to vanish. When Ives looked up, he was startled to see a small farmhouse at the edge of a clearing. He had walked these paths many times and never seen a farmhouse near here. Music drifted from inside the house, perhaps from a wooden flute. The door hung open. A grey cat sat in the doorway and a white rooster strutted in the yard.

The tune, rather than repeating its theme, seemed to continually transform it. The flute must have been crude, with a limited range of notes, but it made a hollow, pleasing tone.

Ives waited and listened. Occasionally a gust of wind rushed up from the valley, bringing the smell of the creek, and then the clattering sound of windblown leaves overpowered the flute. Ives concentrated. His heart beat more rapidly.

He took a step toward the door and the rooster crowed. The music stopped. Ives stopped. For a moment all was quiet in the woods and in the clearing. The cat had disappeared.

"Hello," Ives called. No answer came from the old house. "May I enter?" he asked, as he walked toward the half-open door. No answer.

Ives approached the gray, wooden steps and stood cautiously, weight mostly on his left foot as he peered into the darkness of the open door. There seemed to be no furniture or people in the house.

He whistled the notes of the flute's song, continuing its meandering pattern, in hopes that the flautist might join him.

He found he was trembling. The house, he was suddenly sure, had not been here before. He had walked this part of the woods. This door led somewhere other than a place on earth.

*Am I, once again, a spirit attendant?* Ives thought. He became afraid that if he entered the house, he would not return to the fine summer day, or perhaps to his life at all. He turned and walked briskly toward the valley and the creek. As he walked he spoke the names of his sisters and his parents and his cousins, all deceased now, until he emerged from the trees and the sun warmed his bare forearms, which released a flood of good feeling.

—————————

Had his inner life overwhelmed him? His wife gone, his retirement, the sisters passed away, and for companionship no longer even a dog. Was he inside a kaleidoscope of singing birds and blinding memories? But still, the fine day. The town.

Ives reached the creek, where he stood and listened. The strange house began to recede from the foreground of his mind. Rabbits jumped in the marshy fiddleheads beyond and waterbugs skittered over the top of the pooled water. Under the creek's surface, stones seemed to glow. Among the light-colored stones at the deepest part of the creek, Ives saw something moving. He stepped closer. He didn't know there to be fish this far upstream, though certainly he had seen crayfish.

Sunlight played along ripples on the water's surface, confusing his vision. The sound of the creek continually distracted him, like falling snow. He heard it and heard it, yet it never formed into coherence. He leaned over the deep weight of the creek bed.

The moving thing appeared to be a hand. Ives jumped back and laughed at himself.

He leaned again over the eddying creek and watched the fingers of the underwater hand reach upward. It expanded and contracted. It was a hand. It could not be avoided.

Though it was impossible, Ives immediately thought there must be a person buried under the creek, trying to come out.

He strode into the creek, positioning both feet around the hand, ready to reach down and pull the person up from the creek bed. But the hand shot away, downstream, moving more quickly than anything he had seen before. Ives stood in the creek for a time, dumbfounded. Eventually he realized his feet were cold. He looked down. The mud disturbed by his shoes had already clouded and washed away.

———————

Alone in the sun, awash in the strangeness of the day, he felt acutely that he was not of this place and its people. Their pale silences. Still, he hoped the simple chatter of town might tether him. *Ah, my old friend loneliness*, he thought. He might be trapped in some distorted aspect of it. Sunshine, at least, warmed his face. He felt it soaking in. But it had been a hand.

At the bridge to town Ives felt hungry and said aloud, "I wish I had some lemonade." It was then he noticed a figure on the other side of the bridge. A man, oddly dressed in ragged layers of dark clothing on such a warm June day. The man seemed to be staring intently in the direction of Ives.

"Hello there!" Ives called out.

The man nodded and otherwise made no move to change his bearing. This gave Ives a feeling of trepidation, and he dallied before crossing the bridge. He stopped and peered tentatively into the creek, listening to its voice again and watching as runoff brought dislodged leaves and twigs and husks down through the woods, to where the creek joined the river proper. He stepped partially off the gravel road, testing the embankment, which felt spongy and led steeply down to the creek banks and the underside of the rusted bridge. When he looked up, the man continued watching in stillness.

"Are you in need sir?" Ives said. He didn't know why he said exactly that. It had come out on an impulse.

The man did not change his posture or his intent staring.

Ives stared up at a passing cloud. He felt vexed. Singing Woods was known to vex, but he was no child. Though perhaps he was passing to a second childhood, as he had seen his father pass unknowingly to an imbecility not without its charms. The cloud above him seemed almost to take the form of a rabbit.

When he looked down, the man was at his side. How rapidly and without sound the man had moved. Ives examined the man's face.

"I wonder," the man said, with an unnerving buzz in his voice, "if you have considered the spirit today."

"Oh certainly," said Ives. He stepped around the man but not as if to avoid him. Rather, he motioned with an angling of his head that the man should walk with him back across the bridge, and they began, and the man's feet seemed to touch so lightly on the gravel road that Ives could not hear his steps. He danced, or perhaps floated across their little bridge.

As they walked, Ives felt compelled to talk. Not to dispel discomfort, rather he felt an almost magnetic pull on the thought and language in his mind toward its expression. It was the stranger, the spring day, the sound of the creek, the rabbit-shaped cloud, the unexplainable phenomena from the morning—the unexplainable universes all around.

He told the man his story. His life growing up in nearby Farmington, and the accident that had taken his sisters, and his years working on farms before going off to State college, and the tidy job he had found teaching music and conducting the high school band. The bells kits, the old pianos, the rickety trombones. All of that part had been wonderful. He had once owned a horse. He had briefly loved his wife, mismatched as they had been, and he told the man how they had separated and been strangers to each other for many years, her life far away in Missouri now only the occasional subject of reverie.

The bridge seemed to span his deepest memories.

As they walked, the man began to hum a tune from deep in his throat. Sunlight reached them occasionally. Ives' shoes had nearly dried. He listened intently to the man's idle humming in concert with the wind in the leaves and the insects hovering over the creek. He enjoyed the sounds immensely. They walked in step with each other and with the season's growing intensity.

Small birds swooped down to survey the creek or bathe quickly in its shallow eddies. Ives realized the man was humming the same mutating tune the flautist had played earlier in the farmhouse.

It *was* the same tune.

"I must leave you, sir," Ives said, looking straight ahead. The man continued his humming. "No, I'm sorry, I must leave you now."

They had been walking for a long time, across a strange bridge. A seemingly endless bridge, yet familiar. The creek gushed below; the branches filled with leaves above. The dusty gravel.

"I am leaving you now sir." Ives did not look at the man. He felt as though his life now depended on not looking at this man. On making a clean break.

Had it been days since they started across the bridge? Had this man been trying to reach him with his music earlier? Since Wasioja even? He walked quickly and with purpose, until he began to trot, and there came a break from the grip of the bridge, a feeling of release, and the man's strange song faded behind. He still did not look back, relieved when the song was out of earshot, and took no chances with the stranger.

He emerged from the shady bridge, alone, and hurried toward town. There was the bleak, sunny parking lot of the restaurant. There was the Friendly Tavern. There was the sheriff's station and the old opera house. He did not look back.

———————

So this was the life of the cursed. The afflicted. It was lonelier still at the source of incoherence. He crossed the road and walked a half-block to main street, a short strip of limestone buildings from the mid-1800s.

He did not know what to make of his feelings of dread and thought to check his box at the post office. The mail itself was inconsequential, though he loved the little windows and the painted numbers and the odd brass combination locks for each tiny door. He stopped and considered this, then turned back, in fear for the safety of his pure feelings.

What song had floated from the dance hall of his childhood when he saw the man in suspenders? The Clarinet Polka? Blue Skirt Waltz?

A crow shrieked for a time from its perch atop the light pole.

He saw a sandwich board advertising a quilt show at the opera house. The sign promised lemonade and a cool dark room and dust from old beams settling onto the waxed floor.

He entered, holding his famished belly, and waited for his eyes to adjust. He already knew these rooms as ghost-filled and molded over, the faded stage fit for melodramas, the silent rows of sprung theater seats yawning along. Years of familiarity hadn't eased the room's time-capsuled peculiarity.

He turned in a circle and surveyed the quilt show. Then he stopped and stood as still as possible. A small round woman with graying hair sat behind a wooden desk. She gestured toward the quilts.

"These quilts were all made in Dodge County. Some of them are over a hundred years old." She looked closely at him. "Are you alright?" Her nametag read simply: Ruth.

Ives hadn't moved. He said, "I'm having a strange day. Is there still lemonade?" The breeze from long ago at the farmhouse revived itself in dim remnants and fluttered into the room. It felt in its soft clapping to be the same breeze, in any case.

Certainly people died from curses every day.

Ruth narrowed her eyes. "Each of these quilts is a spiritual document," she said, getting up from behind the desk and walking toward him. They were the only two in the building, perhaps, and her voice echoed.

The quilts were displayed on standing quilt racks in a semi-circle behind the theater seats. Twelve in all. They reminded Ives of a clock, and he said so.

A cloud crossed over the sun outside, and the room dimmed. He felt an awareness of the vast powers surrounding every little detail of life.

"Forget time," Ruth said brusquely, then caught herself. "I have named these quilts myself. I printed up each little tag. This one is *streams of blood overflowing the four rivers*. This one *the formation of the immaculate womb*. This one *hand of god reaches through the water*."

Ives stood still before the quilts and the word *uncanny* came to him as if deposited into his brain through a slot by a mechanical arm. He was having an *uncanny* day. He stared at the woman as she spoke.

"Do you see the hand?" she asked, gesturing toward the quilt with her eyes. He looked and saw only a geometric pattern.

"I would like a glass of lemonade," he said absent-mindedly.

Sunlight gradually returned to the room and warmed its dust. Ruth stepped very close to him and searched his face.

"How pale you are," Ruth said. He perceived a change of temperature in the room. She leaned confidentially toward him and said, "You are probably just some kind of ghost sucked out of Hades through a straw in a frozen daiquiri. I'm kidding." Now he looked at her more closely as well. She hissed at him, "And look at your shoulder. What kind of demon brings a moth into a quilt show? I must ask you to leave."

Ives stepped back. He looked to his left shoulder and sure enough, a small white moth sat on the cloth of his shirt, its wings flat. He felt overcome by its trusting companionship. He could not hear its wings, yet he knew their song to be patient with beauty.

"I'm sorry," he said, "I'm sorry for everything." He stared for a moment at the next quilt, with its grey cat and white rooster. "Come along, my friend," he whispered to the moth. He suddenly felt proud that he had reached for the hand in the creek.

———————

As he walked, Ives remembered that whenever it rained, his mother used to say "God is present." He never asked her what she meant, and now it was too late. Could a curse be a form of spiritual awakening? Hadn't Moses and Muhammed at first suffered from the burden of being chosen? He wasn't sure. The moth had flown away.

To his right, the river itself seemed an impossible wonder, and the park, with its stone benches, and the fish, living out their lives somewhere below. Cottonwood trees released thousands of seeds through the air, held aloft by a parachute of white fibers. A cloud weighing a million pounds floated over his head. A wolf spider worked and worked along the rim of a metal trash can, leaving behind a hundred eggs. Nothing around him seemed feasible. It was all miracles, simple as an effusion of cottonwood seeds through late June sunlight near a river or as staggering as the global movement of water through rivers and clouds and the roots of trees and the blood of insects.

And what did this do for loneliness? Even divine interconnectedness, what good was it, beyond the abstract idea of kinship?

Ives turned toward home, giving up on the town. He walked the long, curved gravel road in the afternoon sun and avoided the shortcut through Singing Woods, the sudden farmhouse, its flute. If spiritual awakening was communion with a larger mystery, then it *was* common as rain, he thought. Each being showed its spirit in a constant web of miracle. Or curse. Was the perception of each being a potential awakening? Hadn't Wordsworth and Blake implied this? He wasn't sure. He heard music when he thought about it. The Blue Skirt Waltz. He saw his mother dancing, and his uncles, and his sisters. His friend today had been the moth, singing on his shoulder. That was enough. There were no miracles.

He walked over the creek again, its water here fed through a cement culvert below a different, smaller bridge. He was alone but he was surrounded. Earth rose to him. A greeting filled with mushrooms.

He saw a deer, a young doe, standing near the creek and slowed to observe it. The deer behaved strangely, kneeling on its spindly forelegs. It seemed to be in pain. Ives stopped and stood at the edge of the road, facing the animal. Its long mouth stretched open as it knelt there. It gasped.

Then he saw the miracle. The deer, as if evaporating, emitted a long stream of text from the skin of its body, in strange black letters, streaming upward to the sky. He gasped at this too, in concert with the deer. Their mouths struggled together.

Was the deer aware of the message, or was it simply releasing pain? Was it poetry? He stepped closer, down through the long weeds of the ditch and up to the barbed-wire fence. He tried to read the text. Clouds crossed over; wind waved the flowered tops of thistles. The letters streamed too quickly or were jumbled. They seemed printed onto a film of invisible light that rose to the clouds.

The message had arrived, but the words were garbled and they streamed from the deer in a language too complex for Ives. He felt how each being walked in a curse *and* a miracle, no closer to truth but constantly a vessel for some larger message, exhausting and unidentifiable. The loneliness of this.

He parted the barbed wire and stepped through. He heard again the voice of the creek but ignored its call. The deer gulped and watched Ives with one wide eye. He believed he could walk near the deer and comfort it.

He spoke softly, "No miracles, it's ok, no more miracles," holding out his palm and trying to soothe her, even as he glanced to identify the letters streaming away. A capital L, perhaps, and a T or a cross, a small zero. It all moved too quickly and was soon lost in the great height of summer.

As Ives crossed into the deer's sensory field, she stood abruptly and the letters stopped. They both paused for a moment and watched each other. Then the deer turned and leapt away.

———————

He stood at the edge of the long uphill field nearest his house, not far from the spot where the hand had appeared in the creek. He didn't dare look there. To his right, a dome of cut and stacked firewood sat near an oak tree. Next to it stood a logsplitter made from an old tractor engine attached to a metal eyebeam, with a hydraulic cylinder mounted onto the beam. The sight of it and the thought of human ingenuity tired him.

He looked to his little home, his refuge. A hawk circled above the field, eyes cast over the living. After a miracle, nothing was different. Butterfly weed bent in the breeze and gathered itself back. Birds rushed to swollen berries. Truly, what was the difference between a curse and a miracle?

He trudged up the hill, up the driveway, past the little outbuildings announcing his patch of countryside. The strangeness of his house, its futuristic presence, frightened him. Late afternoon sun angled through leaves. He passed through the yard and felt he knew each twig and each blade of grass beneath him and that they were strange to him also; it was both strange and known, a world of magic. The eaves and insects and birds of the hill all knew him in return. The deer somewhere licked itself and wondered.

Then his chair, finally his chair, and the sounds of the house. His legs vibrated from the walk and the colors of the walls seemed strange.

He was thirsty. "I'd like a glass of lemonade," he said, as a joke to himself.

He stood and visited the weird land of the kitchen. All the fashioned work of culture arranged neatly in the cupboard. He opened the refrigerator door and took out a can of soda and a bowl of potato salad, then sat heavily at the table and ate.

It was Saturday. Nearly evening.

The refrigerator hummed in electric cycles, and in the sound he heard again theme and variation, perhaps like Bartok but not quite, more like something otherworldly and alien. He drank straight from the tacky opening in the soda can and listened.

He came to realize it was the repeating tune. Ives smiled to himself and thought how light from the nearest star filtered through the maple leaves and the windowpane and landed on his fork and mouth and bowl. The song of his curse continued.

He went to the piano. It was like Bartok, true. He tried to play along but the tune did not find its home on the logical scales of the piano. It evaded him. He began to play Blue Skirt Waltz instead. He sang the few words he remembered: *You thrilled me with strange delight, then softly you stole away.*

Evening came on. He rummaged in the basement for his paints and stepstool. He took these to the front door and looked to the lintel above. He placed the stepladder on his front stoop and the black paint and paintbrush atop it.

Perhaps the same hawk circled still over the valley. He could not tell.

He climbed the stepladder and held the paintbrush then dipped it into the black paint. He saw an ant, solitary and climbing the side of his house. Such work. Then he wrote in a tiny script over his front door, for anyone who climbed up to look closely, "house of miracles."

Soon it would be night. He put his materials away and cleaned his dishes. He took his clothes off and lay down on top of his bedspread in the waning light, aware of his connection to all beings in the valley, yet as alone as ever. He felt the terror of being alive and knew he would not sleep for many hours. Strange tunes passed through his mind and he hummed along with them. He would live his trembling life inside a curse, as would we all, and sometimes he would be able to forget it, and this would be the miracle.

# THE WESTERN STORY

## BOOKS THAT SPEAK TO YOU

He had been reading Western novels at night and for a while it had been calming. He'd set up a special reclining chair in the corner of his grandmother's house and put the old standing lamp with the yellow shade next to it and a stack of his grandfather's paperbacks on the floor nearby and he took time each night to read. He knew it was wrong. Everything in the novels was wrong. Everything about the chair, about his grandfather, everything about his grandfather's death and then his grandmother's and the small linoleumed kitchen and olive-green carpeted living room. It was wrong but it calmed him for a time as he sat and read the tales of genocidal violence in the cone of yellow light and tried not to weep for everything, for his grandmother and her sisters and for America and the Lakota and the Comanche and mostly he tried not to weep for himself.

## THE NEXT STAR

In one of the books a character, the hero, had been attacked and then abandoned to his fate in the high desert with no water. It was a clear night. Sounds of vague animal life arose as he lay broken in the oncoming darkness. And then the hero saw that a strange bright star had emerged on the horizon and that it seemed to pulse, and as he lay bleeding and forcing the broken bones in his arm to meet back up, tying a makeshift splint with his kerchief, the hero felt a calm descend onto him and wondered if it might be the calm of death, and if this strange star might be the vehicle of transmission to the heavens.

And at this he felt compelled to consider that he himself reading in the cone of light might be inside the starry vehicle of transmission where only days earlier his grandmother had moved on, and that the calm arising in him from the paperbacks might actually be the calm of death, settling into him as well, so he stopped reading for the night.

## THE EASIER PATH

The easier path, he thought, led away from grief. In the novels, whoever took the shortcut through the mountain pass to save a day or even a few hours before darkness settled over the ridge, would later be found near a wagon or at the edge of a path as a charred or partially dismembered body and this was always the result of choosing the easier path. But how does one choose to walk directly into oncoming difficulty, its long path, its prolonged doubt? The hero was meant to demonstrate the fortitude required for necessary acquiescence to suffering, and occasionally the books implied this ability to be inherent in his character, and it seemed to him in the moment of his loss that these heroes demonstrated the value of surrender, despite their stoicism.

## VISITORS AT MIDNIGHT

After a few days of solitary meals and reading Western novels and taking care of the plants and cleaning out shelves and repair work with a sack of patch concrete in the damp basement, he heard a knock at the door. He was just settling in to his evening routine, certain he could regain its efficacy. His cousin Jim stood at the door, leaning forward to peer through its rectangular upper window, hands in his pockets. He wore glasses now. He had a belly. But still the same goofy smile and an old Def Leppard t-shirt. He waved Jim in, and they stood awkwardly in the kitchen, until he remembered to offer a beer or some water or he could make a cup of tea.

Jim gratefully accepted the beer, and he opened one for himself as etiquette demanded.

"Just kind of wanted to check in. Heard you were staying here after Auntie Lois died."

"Thanks. Just putting some things in order, really. Going through the little stuff."

They updated each other there at the kitchen table, on the last seven or eight years. They were family and they didn't have to be close or even to like each other in order to assume a level of intimacy.

"Let me show you what I've been trying to do," he said, and led Jim down to the basement, where they stood beneath the bare bulb staring at the drying section of patched wall.

"Did you change the grade on the outside?"

"Yep."

"What about this spot over here?"

He hadn't noticed it.

They worked together for a while, mixing up a new batch to repair the wall, and drank two more bottles of beer each, until the six-pack was gone and the job was roughly finished, relieved to have a subject they could understand.

"Job's not done until the cleanup's done," Jim said, and he carried the tools over to the laundry sink. Now, since reading the Westerns, Jim reminded him of a mule carrying sacks of gold across a mountain pass, doomed to suffer ambush but presently oblivious to anything but the immediate struggle for sure footing.

Back in the kitchen, Jim asked for a glass of tap water. Then he said, "Well, death is normal. It's not pathological. There is no answer to it. It's not a problem to solve."

He agreed.

It was midnight when Jim finally said goodbye. They shook hands, closer than they had been when Jim entered, able to at least touch each other.

He stood on the porch and watched Jim walk to the car, past a small cloud of fireflies electrifying the quiet yard. He wondered if Jim was a ghost.

## CLUES IN THE HILLS

Back in the novels, a pair of identical twins lived in the same county and one of them was wreaking havoc under the other's name, while the innocent twin tried to clear himself, and a shady real estate plot related to the railroad unfolded in the background. But he couldn't seem to stay awake. He knew it was the beer and got up to make some black tea. He wanted to get past the moment and resume his search, as he had come to think of it, in this strange world of men following invisible codes and carrying guns and espousing cutthroat philosophy. He reclined in the chair and opened the book, his teacup on a knit doily beside him, and the novelist seemed to have written *The great ridge hung like a crust of bread over the town, to be dipped into its steaming entrails.* He put the book down. He thought briefly of sugar beets and of garden snails and of the small packets of scented herbs his grandmother kept in the dresser drawers. He felt the reverse of urgency. He drifted. Then he resumed course, sipped his tea, and reopened the book. The author seemed to have written *This divine attention to the smallness of life could be fascism or it could be poetry.*

When he looked up, his grandmother sat on the couch near him, staring expectantly into his eyes.

"I think you're my husband," she said.

"No, I'm your grandson." He was happy to see her. That was his first feeling, before the disbelief and discomfort.

"No, I think you're my husband."

"I'm not. I'm just in his chair."

She smiled.

Lois looked around the room a moment then returned her gaze to his face. "Ruins. A life in ruins is less romantic than a building. Your little patch in the basement was sweet, but what can it do. Look at you. Here you sit. My husband. Just like always. The searcher who never leaves his chair!"

Lois smoothed the lap of her wrinkled dress.

Deep night descended on the town, croaking and dark with its wet gardens sagging under dewy weight.

"I'm your grandson, I'm getting the house ready."

"Ready for what?" she snapped.

He didn't speak. He stared back at her.

She looked at him with a glimmer of spite and said, "There is no answer to it." Just as Jim had said.

Then she was gone.

His tea still steamed in its cup on the doily. A june bug bounced heavily along the window outside, trying to reach the living room light.

He stood up. The book had fallen to the floor. The title of the book was Twin Outlaws of Demon Gulch. He went to the bathroom and washed his face with a cold washrag.

There was no answer, and he was no husband.

## GHOST ADDRESS

As he roamed and worked and paced and waited in the cramped house, he became aware of a surrounding house. As if time-shadowed now by past attachments, the house he had moved out of, or rather been thrown out of, still echoed in faint dimensions, dark and beyond, in the present rooms where he lay thinking. Which is to say a haunted shell hovered above. He heard its vaporous cabinet doors and window weights and light switches moving in phantom echoes. He imagined this house superimposed over, or more often hovering slightly above, Lois' house.

One rainy night when he was still married he had met an ex-lover for drinks and afterward they made out in the steamed car in the parking lot, thinking themselves isolated by the rain and fogged windows, and loosened morally by cocktails and by pheromonal remembrance of past embraces and by desperation for any equal force pressing back, acknowledgment of the need for blind sensation, a need that had long ruled his life. From slam dancing to snorting to mainlining to affair after affair, nothing brought him to fullness.

He had landed here, rather than the hospital, mostly out of timing and circumstance, and had in fact been quite close to taking his life in order not to simply face and correct the person he had become. In the paneled offices of lawyers and therapists everything he knew about himself had crumbled away, so that now, the false past in tatters behind and the unimaginable future ahead equally shredded, only the interminable present remained, reeking with a discomfort that edged him awake at night. The normal question of existence remained just out of reach.

So he stood and looked out the side window at the dark, spent street and thought always of the windows of that other house, half looking through them still, seeing an outline of red maples guarding the sidewalk and the tranquil shade garden as it filled with slowly heaving shoots.

## ANIMAL LIFE

He kept on, each night, with the Westerns. In the next book a strange animal had been haunting the camp of a group of ranchers. At the same time, a caravan of unknown and mysterious people had been working their way across the high plains, leaving in their wake a trail of bones and boots. The animal's prints were too large; its sounds unfamiliar. The hero of the story decided that to solve the mystery he must apply divine reason to the smallness of life: to the minute world of the paw print's impression near the creek bed; to the scents and sounds drifting above the spied-upon caravan; to the crass comebacks from barroom men and women of Dodge Center and the secretive farmers of Plainview.

He read in the creaky chair, alarmed and bewildered by the appearance of the ghost. He tried to dismiss it as a dream, but also—he didn't want to abandon his grandmother. The strange animal circled closer, and the voyeuristic hero watched as the caravan encountered the beast. The beast, of course, communicated with the caravan. It was unclear whether it did their bidding or the reverse. The hero simply watched. At one point he had the opportunity to burn down the caravan and the beast at once and did not. Eventually, the beast escaped into distant, unfamiliar hills devoid even of geography. The caravan would travel on, endlessly it seemed, across one border after another. The hero was left standing near a trail of grotesque footprints, leading nowhere, and he turned back, unaware that now the beast was watching him.

He looked up from the novel and considered: Maybe a ghost was a projection, but maybe he had been summoned, and perhaps kept here, by the ghost. Who was doing whose bidding? Certainly services existed that would take care of the house for a portion of the sale. His throat grew dry. Certainly he was no longer a husband, especially to a ghost. He got up and looked in the refrigerator, then closed the door. He listened but heard only the humming of the refrigerator's motor as it struggled to regain itself.

He returned to the solace of the novel's forward motion. On the ride home, the hero was attacked by the beast. A simple ambush on the dark trail. First the unspeakable scent, then the largeness of the shadow and the too-quick movements. The hero had been foolish to believe he could watch the caravan unnoticed. Its uncanny communication extended far beyond his basic senses.

The beast scared his horse, and he flew, injuring his left knee. But he managed to pull his gun and fire three shots, two into the beast's right paw, leaving it blown apart and dangling. The beast retreated; the hero passed out.

The hero awoke the next day in a bed above the doctor's office, the doctor tending his knee and his head. As he lay on the cool office cot, the doctor absent-mindedly told him of an odd young woman from the caravan whose mangled hand he had amputated that morning. It had been shot through twice and hung shattered and limp. The strange girl, a beauty the doctor said, couldn't speak.

## ABANDONMENT

The phone was still in order but hadn't rung once in his time there.

Robins skittered across the lawn, hunting worms. Grass bent in waves of wind. This interlude in the house held the texture of mirage. He could not quite see it but knew himself to be inside it. Once long ago he had abandoned himself and to the resulting emptiness he had continually applied sensation. Now in the quiet house there came no pleasures, no gratification, no heightened crossing of taboo to help him feel that he existed. The house emanated indwelling, its purpose the vehicle for a spirit. He wandered in its residue.

Cars passed seldom enough that he watched to see if he knew the driver. He had put the book down long ago; it was all propaganda. Time, when slowed, grew lush with boredom. He went into the bathroom where the medicine cabinet door hung open so he wouldn't see himself. The song of sleep, the unlit universal lullaby, crept to his mind. The bathtub echoed nothing. One lost hour after another.

A ghost house might ever hover over him, eventually aim him toward dementia. He thought of Jim, the mountain pass, the sacks of gold.

## BEING SAVED

He had been avoiding the garage, having glanced only once at the dusty windows and angled frame and set off quickly toward the garden. He knew almost nothing of the garage. He did not remember ever being inside it. He knew that his aunt had once hidden there to smoke cigarettes as a teenager. He knew that his grandfather had once hung a pig from the rafters and slaughtered it.

It had been years since it had functioned as anything other than a storage shed. It appeared too narrow for modern vehicles. It leaned south.

He lay on the quiet bed, in the attic bedroom, profoundly alone. He had been officially divorced for only six months but had been separated for a time before that. He thought of the gray coin he often saw when trying to consider both sides of an idea. He would imagine a large coin, in space, slowly rotating by its own power. For example, one side of the coin of this moment would be recuperation, healing, attention to details, family, work, forward progress. The other side would be hiding out, avoidance, regression, the inability to face his shame. The coin spun through his mind space and he watched it recede into darkness. He saw it often.

Today he would conquer the garage. That seemed enough, though for all he knew, it was not possible. On the other side of that coin was simply leaving it alone, doing nothing, selling the house as is.

He heard sounds in kitchen. The tap ran then a pan scraped along a burner grate. A cupboard door opened and closed. He wasn't afraid. No one was sneaking up on him. There was just someone in the house. He reluctantly rose from bed, hoping simply that it wasn't his ex-wife.

He dressed before he called down the stairwell, "Hello?" No answer came so he walked slowly sideways down the staircase with his back pressed against the wall, peering as far as he could around the corner.

When he came in sight of the kitchen he saw Lois, one hand on her hip and one holding a teakettle. "What would you like for breakfast?" she said.

"Why are you here? Or how?"

"It's still my house," she said. "What would you like?"

"Fried eggs on toast," he said automatically.

He sat down at the table and watched her efficient, procedural movements. The morning still thin. Lois removed the carton of eggs from the refrigerator and unwound the coated wire clasping shut the bread bag.

"I'm just having tea. And toast with honey. It's so early."

Outside the small town sat still as a nest. Leaves shone. No cars yet.

"A summer morning," said Lois, "can actually feel kind of like a threat."

"What's in the garage?" he asked.

"How should I know?" Lois snapped. "You're the one who's 'getting it ready'."

He stood and walked to the door and looked out the high rectangular window, to the tilted garage. He realized his back was to her, and it made him uneasy. Who ever turned their back on a spirit, or even a hallucination?

"Don't mess with the garage," she said quietly, her voice whistling and reedy.

"Why not?"

When he turned back she was gone. The burner was unlit. He was hungry, and thought to cook the eggs.


## THE GARAGE

The garage door was a strange wooden folding panel affair, locked through a metal loop and slat by a combination lock that had rusted over. He went to the basement and brought out a pry bar, inserting its sharp flat head beneath the metal slat by depressing the soft wood of the frame; he pressed down on the pry bar until the slat gave way.

The garage door moved a little, and from inside the wormy smell of dirt and rust rose up at the touch of spring air. His eyes filled with shadows, the one window covered with cardboard. He was surprised to find it tidy, and mostly empty.

With his full weight he pushed the folding door a bit further, hoping for more light, then pulled down the cardboard to reveal the four-paned window. Dust circled in sudden brightness. He saw the homemade workbench fashioned from leftover 2x4s and plywood. A rope and pulley hung on an old square nail on the west wall. A cracked washing machine hose on the east wall, and a can of ancient paint below the workbench. No tools. On the workbench one small dusty clump, potentially animal and long dead, in the darkness. He stayed back. In the rafters above, some 2x10 planking and a bicycle wheel. Air from long ago.

But it had already registered. He moved a cautious step closer to the workbench. He had known the desiccated lump in a second. He moved another further step and peered as if over a ledge. There sat a peaceful and dried human left hand. He stepped out, went to the apple tree and found an old branch on the ground. He returned to the garage and stood a few feet from the bench; he poked the hand with the stick.

The hand wobbled exactly as it should. He observed the garage more closely and nothing else seemed sinister. He felt he should be more alarmed. Someone long ago had experienced the separation of their hand from their arm. That was all he could know of it. The person he needed to ask about the hand was no longer real.

The garage floor had been returning to dirt for years. He closed the door and went for his tools. He would screw the door shut and leave it.


## SINGING WOODS

Across the street a patch of woods began. It had once contained the most mysterious and elegant darkness of his young life. He had fantasized about it often from his grandmother's garden. The relatively mundane and tame edge of Singing Woods abutted Maple Street and the town proper. One August day when he must only have been three years old, or less, he had wandered across the street and into the woods.

When he arrived every subject to which he trained his eye had been startlingly numerous. He remembered bending to see beetles with large pincers growing out of the tops of their heads crawl over decaying leaves. He remembered lifting a small, flat, wet rock to find beneath it a pale worm in its perfectly exposed tunnel. The sodden reek of air passing over long, slow decay.

When he heard the adults calling his name from across the street he crouched and hid. He didn't know why. The presence of the woods enveloped him. He picked up an old bottle cap and studied the mysterious design on its face. The calling grew in pitch and came nearer. He lifted a ragged leaf. A slug lived its life there, underneath.

They found him in his bright clothes and scooped him up like a melon. He watched Singing Woods recede, upside down, pinned to a hip. He was never to do that again. Much later he would hide bottles of schnapps in these woods and make out with other teenagers also desperate for affection. He would wander and smoke, making obscene lists in his head.

## THE HORSE

The book that night told the story of a young greenhorn who learned to rope and shoot while driving a herd of cattle south into Texas. A natural. He grew to challenge the leader of an outfit of cast-off ranch hands for the love of a powerful heiress near Odessa. There was the usual hidden valley. Some high desert bandits drinking moonshine. A gambler. But then he noticed, part way through the otherwise standard story, that the horse belonging to 'the Kid' could talk. *That can't be right*, he thought. He double-checked. The horse's dialogue was no snappier, but it was clearly the horse speaking. At one point the horse said, "Don't worry, Kid. I know men; I know where they'll be."

He stood, the page saved with his left hand, and went to the window. The town was quiet and the streetlamps turned on and off occasionally. Animals talked and rambled, and ghosts, and the night itself made a loud round syllable, too big to hear.

In the kitchen he found a stepstool in the space between refrigerator and wall. He set it and carefully mounted each step to open the small cupboard doors above the refrigerator. Another useless place, suitable mainly for hidden or forgotten things.

The two square cupboard doors opened outward. Inside, poisons of many brands. Powders, mostly. Too many poisons for just mice. He closed the doors. The poisons in the cupboard somehow made the room feel smaller.

Anything could happen day or night now. Far into the morning, he could begin cleaning the oven. He could dream in the middle of the windblown day and the dream might walk in and out of the light. The horse had spoken. The beasts changed shape, and he stood alone and divorced in the kitchen of his childhood.

## INTERROGATION SONGS

He felt the heat of expectation, unable to bring attention to the world in the novel or to memories from his life, even to old addresses and phone numbers and objects. Each thought flew carelessly from awareness. He was between realities again. He wanted to ask her about the hand.

For most of life he had hoped to discern a secret, though the secret had kept changing its host. As a young person he had wanted to understand his place in reality. But later he wanted to know what material he was looking through, what distortions his mind used to shape reality. He had been the least of men for much of life without knowing why. He could not see himself.

He heard Lois moving upstairs, or in fact knew Lois was there before hearing her, by a sudden feeling of sensory amplification. She walked down, carefully placing each foot to each stair, as always. One hand on the wall and one held behind her back.

When she brought her arm from behind her he could see that her left hand was bandaged.

"What happened to your hand?"

She looked at him squarely and said, "I think you did that."

He stepped back as a thought formed in his stomach and made its way up to his mind: *This might not be Lois at all.* Fear rose through him, weakening his limbs. They stood six feet apart while around them beings careened violently, siphoning the life from each other. Light and wings and dust and sound waves, always eating.

"How are you able to visit me?"

Lois Blood looked down and sighed, as if tired of explaining something over and over to a child. "I exist when I think to exist. And that is basically the case for all of us." She crossed her arms, hiding the bandaged hand. "To live is an act of concentration," she said. "Just focusing your energy. It gets harder when your carriage has perished." She turned away and moved toward the open porch door, pausing to listen at the threshold.

They stood together in the hush, both of them concentrating. Then her face lit up and she turned to him, hands behind her.

"I used to sing that song," she said, "about flies in buttermilk. Do you remember that?"

He nodded. He had been fond of her singing as a child and requested many specific songs he thought of as her 'hits.' The sweetness of this memory flooded him for a moment. His smallness and expectation and the names of the songs. The Streets of Laredo. The Green Green Grass of Home. A Daisy a Day.

She frowned and said, "All those songs are trailing behind me now, like a rope."

He stared at her. She seemed as present as anyone that he knew, in her impossible flowered dress. He wanted to ask if she could appear in different clothing at different times but thought the word "appear" might be insulting. He wanted to ask about the hand.

"There was a song about a girl named Cindy," she said. "She had to get on home. Didn't you have a girlfriend named Cindy once?" Her eyes burned into him.

He felt her gaze as a being, a life form binding him there, holding him in place. Around them many crickets, louder than he thought possible. He turned his head to the side so that his good ear was closer to her. She began to sing. "I wish I was an apple, a-hangin' on a tree, and every time lil' Cindy pass'd she'd take a big bite of me..."

He smiled and closed his eyes and listened to her cracked voice. It was like listening to an eggbeater or a woodpecker, how spaces between sounds made the peculiar tone, its personality. The absence. The still point of a reed, before it restarted its vibration. As if the inanimate objects all around could sing or were always singing and passed through her on a dark porch while light treated the faraway world. All of his skin listened too, touched by air from her song.

Then she stopped. "What happened to Cindy? Hmmm? What happened to her?" She said it as if she knew what happened, as if in accusation. She leaned in. "Why are *you* here? Do you know?"

He tried to be unknowing. He guarded his mind from knowing.

Lois approached him with a strange smile. She said, "Did you ever wonder what happened to her little baby? That you never even saw?"

"Oh, yes," he said, "My life formed around that little baby." He swallowed back his tears. "I mean, I formed my fake life around its absence."

"You need a nap, Mikey. It's past your bedtime."

"Sing a little more," he said. But she was fading away.

## THE LOOSE MOORING

In the morning he lay in the narrow bed and listened to Singing Woods move its windblown body and to the chorus of insects from the garden and the bubbling voice of a diesel truck. After breakfast he called the realtor.

Cindy had simply disappeared for a year, the way Catholic girls sometimes did then. And then returned: quiet, sullen, no longer pregnant, kept close by her father. Unavailable to him, at first. But then, occasionally again, the woods, the schnapps, their desperate kissing.

It was loneliness that he knew best, from the beginning. No one had phoned him then or now. To be released of the tipped over hours' uncertain bedside hush, to not crack open in the lingering night, to not descend. It was loneliness and greed. Every partner he'd ever had, two things: he had cheated on them, and gotten them pregnant. Every one. He had, despite appearances, given them nothing.

Once when he was only five years old, a neighbor girl had given him flowers on May Day. She had brought a little bouquet to his door. He didn't know what to do, and in confusion, he ripped up the flowers, said he didn't want them, and sent the girl away.

His grandmother had seen him. She grabbed him by the arm and yanked him into the kitchen. She said, "Never, never treat a girl that way! Never!" There were tears in her eyes. This woman who had been beaten and often abandoned by an alcoholic husband, who raised six children through the depression working as a waitress at a lunch counter. *Never*, she said.

He nothinged along through the day, waiting. It was as if, on a stoppage to replenish himself near a dark lake, he bent to drink and saw his own face filled with hatred.

When the realtor appeared, it turned out he had known her vaguely in high school. She had been two years younger, and they had traveled the same school hallways, shoplifted the same convenience store aisles, driven aimlessly the same county roads. She wore a black polyester blazer and matching skirt. She smiled and said hello, her eyes all over the house, corner to corner, appraising.

He showed her each room, and the garden, and mumbled about the garage not really being worth seeing. Then they stood on the front sidewalk and she mentioned some numbers and some dates and gave him a sheet of paper with names of people to call—inspectors and craftspeople. "Your grandfather was a real son of a bitch," she said.

"What?"

"He fucked a lot of people over. That's probably where you got it. I don't blame you. I'm just here to sell the house."

"Have I?"

"They were my friends. It was a long time ago. Call this inspector; she's the best. I can have it listed in a week."

THE LAST BOOK

He had reached the final novel in the pile. It caught him by surprise. He could always start again of course. There might still be more somewhere. There might be more in the basement pantry. But in truth he had reached the end and the end was uncomfortable.

In the last book, a gruff, heroic cowboy who lived by a code of solitude and independence had been left with a small lamb by a couple heading further west. *Just watch her while we get our horse, please,* they begged. *We'll never make it back in time with her.*

If they didn't come back, the hero planned to roast the lamb.

Then the hero met a preacher, who spoke to him of the lamb. The preacher peered into its mouth and ran his hands over the lamb's skin. "An innocent beast, a sea of nerves," he said, and sang a little song to the lamb, so that it followed him around.

The preacher convinced the hero that he would care for the lamb. It was symbolic, he said, it was in the Bible. Then the preacher said, "let your loins be girded about, and your lights burning." Something was off about him, and strange things had gone missing from the nearest town just before he appeared. A sheriff had ridden out to ask the hero about it.

When the couple returned, the hero had given the lamb to the preacher. They took off after their lamb, fixated and wild-eyed, and the cowboy hero followed. He watched from behind a rock as the couple brutally ambushed the preacher, murdered him, and right there on the ground they slit the lamb's belly.

The hero crept closer to see what they were doing and found himself in a shootout, on the verge of demise, cornered and injured, when the sheriff reappeared. Now the couple was ambushed; they lay bleeding and helpless. From inside the lamb's body, the sheriff fished out a small sack of gold. The book was titled *The Body of the Lamb.*

## THE SONG PATH

He woke in the narrow bed, in the dark night, his busy mind listing the final steps to put the house up for sale. He heard singing. He went toward it. Down the steps, onto the porch and out to a starry, moonlit night. Lois, singing from across the street. He followed the song, in his slippers, confused by overlapping and weedy darknesses rising around him.

He saw her on a path toward the bluff overlooking the creek. She turned and put one finger to her lips to shush him, his steps too loud.

Each leaf and twig echoed in the quiet night woods. She became annoyed and frowned but resumed singing. They walked in tandem, twenty yards apart. She turned again to shush him. He held out his hands and pleaded with his eyebrows in apology. There was nothing he could do, he was so loud and heavy, where she was made of light.

Finally she turned, arms folded, and waited. "Come on," she said, impatient with his slowness. He saw in the moonlight her bright and bandaged hand.

"Let's take the shortcut," Grandmother Lois said, and he followed through dense, low branches, ducking or stepping over. She sang again, "Get along home…" and her voice floated through the leaves. Over them the moon. A cloud crept across. Great animals remained watchful in the sky.

"Didn't you bring the hand?" he asked.

Lois turned and said coyly, "You think there's only a hand?" She shook her head. "Come on."

Relief moved through his body in a wave. Sounds of the creek began to mix with her voice. He followed her, deeper into Singing Woods. It seemed to stretch. It seemed to contain time. They walked in.

# ACKNOWLEDGMENTS

Gratitude to the editors of the journals in which some of these stories previously appeared:

*Ninth Letter*: "the western story"
*Revolver*: "how I became a mother"
*Psychopomp*: "the two daughters"; "the story of eating the king"; "the story of henry ford"; "the story of the box"
*South Dakota Review*: "summer story"

And special thanks to Maureen Aitken and Julia Fine for their invaluable feedback on these stories.

JOHN COLBURN is the author of four previous books, most recently *unabandonment* (Spuyten Duyvil, 2021). He lives in St. Paul, MN and is one of the publishers/editors in the Spout Press collective.

## WHAT BOOKS PRESS

### AN IMPRINT OF

### THE GLASS TABLE

### COLLECTIVE

LOS ANGELES

All WHAT BOOKS feature cover art by Los Angeles painter, printmaker, muralist, and theater and performance artist GRONK. A founding member of ASCO, Gronk collaborates with the LA and Santa Fe Operas and the Kronos Quartet. His work is found in the Corcoran, Smithsonian, LACMA, and Riverside Art Museum's Cheech Marin collection.

*As a small, independent press, we urge our readers to support independent publishers and booksellers. This is easily done by visiting our website, WhatBooksPress.com, where you can purchase books directly from us or from Bookshop.org*

## 2025

*Inside the Umber Iris*
**ERIK MANUEL SOTO**
WINNER OF THE GRONK
NICANDRO FIRST BOOK PRIZE
POEMS

*Persistence of Singing Woods*
**JOHN COLBURN**
STORIES

*River of Angels*
**STEPHEN COOPER**
STORIES

*Jukebox*
**PATTY SEYBURN**
POEMS

*zirconium ash*
**JIMMY VEGA**
POEMS

## 2024

*The Manuscripts*
**KEVIN ALLARDICE**
NOVEL

*Father Elegies*
**STELLA HAYES**
POEMS

*Slow Return*
**PAUL LIEBER**
POEMS

*Dreamer Paradise*
**DAVID QUIROZ**
POEMS

*How to Capture Carbon*
**CAMERON WALKER**
STORIES

## 2023

*God in Her Ruffled Dress*
LISA B (LISA BERNSTEIN)
POEMS

*Figures of Wood*
MARÍA PÉREZ-TALAVERA
TRANSLATED BY PAUL FILEV
NOVEL

*A Plea for Secular Gods: Elegies*
BRYAN D. PRICE
POEMS

*Nightfall Marginalia*
SARAH MACLAY
POEMS

*Romance World*
TAMAR PERLA CANTWELL
STORIES

## 2022

*No One Dies in Palmyra Ohio*
HENRY ELIZABETH CHRISTOPHER
NOVEL

*Us Clumsy Gods*
ASH GOOD
POEMS

*Skeletal Lights From Afar*
FORREST ROTH
FLASH FICTION/PROSE POEMS

*That Blue Trickster Time*
AMY UYEMATSU
POEMS

## 2021

*Pyre*
MAUREEN ALSOP
POEMS

*What Falls Away Is Always*
KATHARINE HAAKE &

GAIL WRONSKY, EDITORS
ESSAYS

*The Eight Mile
Suspended Carnival*
REBECCA KUDER
NOVEL

*Game*
M.L. WILLIAMS
POEMS

## 2020

*No, Don't*
ELENA KARINA BYRNE
POEMS

*One Strange Country*
STELLA HAYES
POEMS

*Remembering Dismembrance:
A Critical Compendium*
DANIEL TAKESHI KRAUSE
NOVEL

*Keeping Tahoe Blue*
ANDREW TONKAVICH
STORIES

## 2019

*Time Crunch*
CATHY COLMAN
POEMS

*Whole Night Through*
L.I. HENLEY
POEMS

*Echo Under Story*
KATHERINE SILVER
NOVEL

*Decoding Sparrows*
MARIANO ZARO
POEMS

## 2018

*Interrupted by the Sea*
PAUL LIEBER
POEMS

*The Headwaters of Nirvana*
BILL MOHR
POEMS

## 2017

*Gary Oldman Is a Building
You Must Walk Through*
FORREST ROTH
NOVEL

*Rhombus and Oval*
JESSICA SEQUEIRA
STORIES

*Imperfect Pastorals*
GAIL WRONSKY
POEMS

## 2016

*The Mysterious Islands*
A.W. DEANNUNTIS
STORIES

*The "She" Series:
A Venice Correspondence*
HOLADAY MASON
& SARAH MACLAY
POEMS

*Mirage Industries*
CAROLIE PARKER
POEMS

## 2015

*The Balloon Containing
the Water Containing the
Narrative Begins Leaking*
RICH IVES
STORIES

*The Shortest Farewells
Are the Best*
CHUCK ROSENTHAL
& GAIL WRONSKY
LITERARY COLLAGE/PROSE POEMS

## 2014

*It Looks Worse Than I Am*
LAURIE BLAUNER
POEMS

*They Become Her*
REBBECCA BROWN
NOVEL

*The Final Death of Rock-and-
Roll
& Other Stories*
A.W. DEANNUNTIS
STORIES

*Perfecta*
PATTY SEYBURN
POEMS

## 2013

*Brittle Star*
ROD VAL MOORE
NOVEL

*Sex Libris*
JUDITH TAYLOR
POEMS

*Start With A Small Guitar*
LYNNE THOMPSON
POEMS

*Tomorrow You'll Be One of Us*
GAIL WRONSKY,
CHUCK ROSENTHAL
& GRONK
ART/LITERARY COLLAGE/POEMS

## 2012

*The Mermaid at the Americana
Arms Motel*
A.W. DEANNUNTIS
NOVEL

*The Time of Quarantine*
KATHARINE HAAKE
NOVEL

*Frottage & Even As We Speak*
MONA HOUGHTON
NOVELLAS

*West of Eden:
A Life in 21ˢᵗ Century Los Angeles*
CHUCK ROSENTHAL
MAGIC JOURNALISM

## 2010

*Master Siger's Dream*
A.W. DEANNUNTIS
NOVEL

*Other Countries*
RAMÓN GARCÍA
POEMS

*A Giant Claw*
GRONK
ESSAY BY GAIL WRONSKY
SPANISH TRANSLATION
BY ALICIA PARTNOY
ART

*Coyote O'Donohughe's
History of Texas*
CHUCK ROSENTHAL
NOVEL

*So Quick Bright Things*
GAIL WRONSKY
BILINGUAL, SPANISH TRANSLATION
BY ALICIA PARTNOY
POEMS

## 2009

*Bling & Fringe
(The L.A. Poems)*
MOLLY BENDALL &
GAIL WRONSKY
POEMS

*April, May, and So On*
FRANÇOIS CAMOIN
STORIES

*One of Those Russian Novels*
KEVIN CANTWELL
POEMS

*The Origin of Stars
& Other Stories*
KATHARINE HAAKE
STORIES

*Lizard Dream*
KAREN KEVORKIAN
POEMS

*Are We Not There Yet?
Travels in Nepal,
North India, and Bhutan*
CHUCK ROSENTHAL
MAGIC JOURNALISM

WHAT
BOOKS
PRESS

LOS ANGELES